Shadow and Flame
Part 2

A COLLECTIVE NOVEL

Elias Raven

The Collective is here…

We've set the stage, created the characters, and fashioned a world full of twists and turns. Now it's your turn to sit back and immerse yourself in this incredible series. Each episode weaves the characters and storylines of five standalone novels together to give you an epic crossover series. We've left you breadcrumbs, tidbits of information intertwined throughout our stories. Can you find them? Can you collect the clues we've left and become part of The Collective and solve the case?

Season One
Featured authors in order of appearance…

International bestselling author -Riley Edwards
www.rileyedwardsromance.com

International bestselling author - Erin Trejo
www.authorerintrejo.weebly.com

Best Selling author - Ellie Masters
www.elliemasters.com

Award winning author - Elias Raven
www.eliasraven.com

Award winning author - Chris Genovese
www.eroticmayberry.com

Best Selling author - Carver Pike
www.carverpike.com

Connect with The Collective at…

Newsletter - http://eepurl.com/cxCJFb

www.TheCollectiveNovels.com

https://www.facebook.com/TheCollectiveNovels

Copyright © 2017 by Elias Raven

Cover design: The Collective
Written by: Elias Raven
Published by: Elias Raven

Shadow and Flame – Part 2

First edition – October 2017
Copyright 2017 Elias Raven

ISBN-13: 978-0-9990237-3-0
ISBN-10: 0-9990237-3-X

Dedication

This novel is dedicated to my online and real world family and friends that have stood by me patiently as this novel has come to fruition. In many ways, this story is the culmination of a dream. I hope you enjoy the world that I have created as much as I enjoyed bringing it to reality.

Thank you all for believing in me.

Acknowledgments

Let me start off by thanking my fellow authors that are involved in The Collective Project: Riley Edwards, Erin Trejo, Ellie Masters and Chris Genovese/Carver Pike. Working through a ten book series with all of you, has been nothing short of a miracle. Thank you so much for your tireless work, late night conversations, and collaborative efforts to make this project come alive.

I would like to thank my Alpha Readers (you know who you are) for all of your help as I put the second book together. I would also like to thank my PA, Kendall Blackburn and friend and fellow co-author Riley Edwards for all of their tireless work and for putting up with me as I pieced together my second novel. Without their help the final draft would not have been completed. Thank you also to Chris Genovese for working with Kendall on tweaking certain parts of this novel, so that the final book flowed better with the end of the series. Thank you to Eva Poole my friend and partner in crime these many years for all of her help formatting and tweaking to get this book ready for publication. Thank you to Michelle L PA for all of her tireless work that she has done for all of the authors in The Collective Project.

To the entire Collective Beta Team, you rock! Thank you so much for all of your constructive feedback and suggestions that helped to make this story the best that it could be. Your efforts are truly appreciated, and none of us could have done this without you.

A big thank you to my street team, The Ravenettes, for all of your hard work promoting the new book and The Collective as a whole. Your enthusiasm and support has kept a smile on my face throughout the whole process.

I would like to give a special shout out to Riley Edwards for all of her work that she has done for The Collective as a whole. I would also like to thank Ellie Masters for planting the seeds that were the genesis of this story and for her continued support & friendship. You have both gone above and beyond to bring this project to life.

I want to give a very special thank you to my friend and mentor, Author Gina Whitney, for allowing me the singular honor of having four of her characters in this book. If it hadn't have been for a chance meeting with this wonderful woman and a reading of *Saving Abel*, I would have never taken pen to paper and written my first novel.

Last, but not least, I would like to thank my fans in The Raven Cave. Without you, this journey would not have been possible. To all of you reading this work for the first time, enjoy the ride...

Chapter 1

~East Coker~

In my beginning is my end. In succession
Houses rise and fall, crumble, are extended,
Are removed, destroyed, restored, or in their place
Is an open field, or a factory, or a by-pass.
Old stone to new building, old timber to new fires,
Old fires to ashes, and ashes to the earth
Which is already flesh, fur, and faces,
Bone of man and beast, cornstalk and leaf.
Houses live and die: there is a time for building
And a time for living and for generation
And a time for the wind to break the loosened pane
And to shake the wainscot where the field mouse trots
And to shake the tattered arras woven with a silent
motto.

Excerpt from Four Quartets by T.S. Eliot

Royston~ "What the fuck is that?" Rhianna said as Misty gasped while pointing at the window. We all turned to look at the dining room window, following her finger. We all saw the words scrawled on the fog-laden glass. The effect was eerie as the fog billowed along the sides of the house and all around us.

"We All Fall Down?" Detective Logan said with hint of question lingering in the air.

Reid looked at all of us and shook his head. "This is some kind of fucked up shit," he mumbled to himself.

Rhianna and Misty were standing next to each other. They both tensed, and I could tell by their body language that Reid's comment wasn't sitting well with either one of them. Before they decided to cut Reid off at the knees, I interjected into the conversation.

"Reid, you have been here with Detective Logan. We all saw and heard the same thing. There are an awful lot of coincidences that are occurring, not the least of which is the choice of music that whomever or whatever was outside chose to use just now," I said.

Misty interjected herself at that point trying to keep her temper in check.

"Reid, I agree this is fucked up. Seriously, nothing like this has ever happened around here or to us. We live in SAUSA-FUCKING-LITO for Christ's sake! We are talking about a really quiet and private neighborhood. On top of that, we don't give our

11

address out to everyone!" she exclaimed.

Reid paced around and looked over at Logan. The detective was already taking pictures of the window before the sunlight came back and evaporated the image. Since the window was wet when the message was left on the glass, there would be no fingerprints to retrieve. As if on cue, the sunlight broke through the fog, and the sky outside started getting noticeably clearer. Logan walked over to us.

"Look, I don't know what is going on here, but now that the sun is coming out, I suggest we go check things out around the property and see if we can find any clues. You all need to stay right here and do not touch anything.

Rhianna looked at everyone then spoke her mind.

"We understand perfectly, but it is my fucking house. So you won't mind if I join you in the hunt outside to find out if there was some assholes playing a prank on us today. There is a distinct possibility that if I find out that we have been pranked, I might just put a bullet in someone's ass or between their eyes, then I might drag them through the back door and say it was trespassing," she said angrily.

"You don't have any objections, do you, Detective Logan?" Rhianna smiled innocently at the officer.

Both Logan and Reid looked at each other then back at Rhianna.

"You are kidding, right?" Logan asked Rhianna.

"Yes I am, but if someone comes after us, officer, I am going to shoot first and ask questions later," she replied with the slightest edge of venom in her voice.

"Then you won't have any objections when I haul your ass to the precinct in cuffs, will you?" Detective Logan replied back with the cocky grin and wink that you would expect from one of San Francisco's finest alpha cops.

"Fine, we will split up, but no one touches anything. Are we clear on that?"

Everyone nodded and agreed.

"Rhianna, Royston, you two come with me. Misty, go with Reid and check for anything out of place in the house. Reid, call me if you all find any clues. If we don't do this by the book, anything we find will be inadmissible," Logan instructed.

Logan nodded his head and we split up. I went with Logan through the back door along with Rhianna. We started searching the backyard and along the tree line. The property wasn't fenced off per se because it was semi secluded. Rhianna's house was at the end of the cul-de-sac and this allowed her property to be pretty well hidden by the tree line. It had a very rustic feel to it. The sides of the house were fenced off up to the front. She left the back yard open to the woods and the hillsides that rolled down from the back. They went together along each side of the house being careful not to touch anything. I could see that Rhianna had her hand firmly in her jacket pocket grasping her father's .38 special.

I knew Rhianna well enough to know she wasn't kidding in what she had told Detective Logan.

She would shoot to kill and ask questions later. That really did concern me, because I also knew Detective Logan would do just as he said, too. He would not let her go off half-cocked and harm someone either. Detective Logan walked over to me while Rhianna was checking for something beneath a large redwood tree.

Logan pointed at the ground toward the house. He took pictures, showing me where the ground had been disturbed and where there were broken branches like something heavy had snapped them. You could tell that Logan's years growing up on a farm and hunting for his supper were showing. He picked up telltale clues in the brush very quickly.

"If you look across here, most of the leaves and brush haven't been disturbed. That would make sense since most of the people that live back here don't go onto the hillsides or along the tree line. The owners do have to keep it cleared for fire season though, so they usually have someone come through and trim and clear brush prior to the summer. Since we are at the beginning of the year, none of this should have been disturbed. Also these look like fresh breaks," he explained to me. I rubbed my chin watching as he laid it all out for me.

"I know you're a sharp cookie, Royston. Now if

you look at the ground here, see the trail going toward the house?"

I nodded my head.

"You sure it's not something the girls do, maybe they hike back here?" he asked.

I honestly couldn't remember if the girls hiked the back of their property or the neighboring properties or not. It wasn't something we had ever discussed. I preferred giving them their privacy where I could and not to intrude too far into what they liked to do in their off time unless invited.

Logan shrugged his shoulders as Rhianna came over to join us. She pointed back at the redwood tree.

"I found this along the base of that tree, snagged in some of the bark. I took pictures of how I found it," she informed us, showing us the pictures on her phone.

We walked back to the tree, and sure enough, there was some fabric caught at the base of the tree. From the initial look, I suspected cotton fabric, perhaps from a sock.

"Looks like white cotton, perhaps from a sock?" I suggested.

Detective Logan nodded his head in agreement.

"Yeah, that's what I was thinking. I don't see any other fabric, but there are broken branches here and the ground was wet enough that there are also some partial shoe prints in the mud. Unfortunately, nothing concrete enough to give the boys in the lab a call," the detective said while pointing to the area in question.

We all looked at each other as I noticed some footprints that looked slightly off. I pointed it out to both Rhianna and Logan.

"Do you see that over there? There are more disturbances in the brush heading toward the neighboring property," I stated.

Logan took more pictures while we followed along, but soon the brush cleared and the ground was harder and we lost the trail. We made our way back to the girl's house where we found Reid and Misty in the back yard waiting for us.

"Did you guys find anything?" Reid asked.

"No, nothing concrete yet, just bits and pieces. We were wondering if Lady Luck had perchance smiled in your direction," I replied.

Both Reid and Misty shook their heads.

"If it's ok with Detective Logan, I would suggest you two have a look over here behind the house. We did find a few things by that large redwood over there, so don't disturb that area. Also, look across the yard and the back tree line area. There are some footprints that Logan was wondering if they might be yours. We will check the window and sides and see if we see anything else." I told them. Detective Logan nodded in agreement.

Both girls nodded as Reid chimed in. "Hey, I am going to go with the ladies while you two check the sides. I want to ask them about the neighbors and get some info."

I gave Logan the chin up signal and we made our way to the left side of the house first. The window that had been written on was rather high up. Whoever or whatever had done it would have had to be over average in height. I would think they would have to be leaning towards six feet or more in stature unless one was standing on a step stool or plastic bucket. A thorough examination of the soil, however, didn't provide any indication that was the case, so we kept looking further. We looked for any sign of fingerprints on the window ledge. The moisture from the fog along with the abrupt return of the sun wiped out any chance we had to find prints.

The left side gate was unlocked, which was strange. Normally, the girls kept the gates secured. I would have to ask them about that later.

We walked through and continued our examination of the front driveway, but found the cul-de-sac eerily quiet. We walked over to the right side of the house and found that gate also unlocked. . We walked carefully down the side of the house but didn't find any further evidence. We continued walking toward the back of the house and found Reid and the ladies waiting for us in the back yard.

"Did you find anything?" Misty asked.

"Yes as a matter-of-fact I did. Did either of you

leave the side gates unlocked? Also, while we were in the backyard we found footprints along the tree line. Did either of you hike back there?" I asked the girls.

Misty and Rhianna looked at me and shook their heads no.

We all started to make our way back inside. Right near the back steps, Detective Logan caught a small movement on one of the pillars. He found another small piece of fabric. This one was grey and black. I motioned for everyone to stop moving and pointed to the fabric where Logan was already taking pictures. Logan pulled a small plastic bag out of his pocket and carefully retrieved the fabric.

"This is just a suggestion, but why don't we retrieve that other clue as well now that we are done investigating the backyard. You ladies did have a look already right? I asked.

"We can mark off the area and map it if we need too. We probably won't get any detail out of the fabric, but now we have found two pieces," I said holding up two fingers.

We went back into the house. Rhianna made a fresh pot of tea for me and coffee for the guys while the rest of us sat around the table again. We reviewed our notes and Reid suggested they finish the original interview that had been planned before we had any further interruptions.

Rhianna and Misty both looked a little tired, but nodded their head. I got up from the table and went into the kitchen and retrieved a pair of latex cleaning gloves from under the sink. I carefully retrieved the boom box that had been left on the porch. It was an older Panasonic, I slid on the pair of latex gloves I had borrowed and examined the radio in minute detail. The radio even had a button to cause the music to re-loop so it was perfect for what had been intended.

I set the box inside of the door and stepped out onto the front stoop and looked around. The cul-de-sac opened at the end of the driveway. Rhianna had one set of neighbors to her right, and they had a son that loved to play baseball. I had been over more than once when he sent one sailing over the wall and it would hit the roof or garage with a loud bang. Rhianna didn't have it in her to be mean-spirited or derogatory to a child that was having fun, but I was slightly more set in my ways. If a young boy hit a baseball into my garage or copper roof, you could bloody well bet that I would be at the parent's door in moments with their child in tow. Perhaps I was a bit more old-fashioned than most, but that was how I was raised. Maybe that was why I was still single when so many of my peers had already tied the knot and signed their life and manhood away.

They could have it; I would rather be the most eligible bachelor in England than drowning trying to get hitched to soon.

I reviewed all the details that we had gathered so far letting the events play out like a movie in my head. We had some tantalizing clues, but they all indicated, at least in this case, the possibility that Rhianna and Misty were being pranked. It wasn't looking supernatural at the moment. As I started weaving the clues together, mulling over the details, I removed the latex gloves and walked down the driveway toward the neighbor's property. Maybe the young rapscallion Billy had seen something. As I passed the fence line from the street, a pair of young faces looked over at me that appeared to be in hiding. My senses immediately went on alert. I pointed at the boys and asked them to come see me. Billy of course knew me on sight.

"Hi, Mr. Royston!" he said cheerfully. His accomplice was a little more reserved. It took me a moment before I placed the face.

"You live a few more houses down," I said. The boy looked over at me then at Billy before replying and pointing.

"Yeah, I live with my grandparents over there," he admitted.

"You're Jonathan?" I inquired. The boy smiled.

"That would be me," he replied, smiling.

"What are you two scalawags doing out here?" I asked.

"Jonathan poked Billy and said, "Shhhh."

At that point I knew something was up.

"Ok Lads, out with it," I said sternly. Billy

looked at me with his freckled face and then at Jonathan before he spoke.

"I told you that guy wasn't one of their friends," Billy said to Jonathan.

My eyes narrowed as I looked at both boys, but at the same time I took a conspiratorial tone with them both. They knew something, and I didn't want the evidence to slip away.

"Did one of our friends play a prank? There was some strange music and all in the fog and we couldn't figure out what it was? Do you know what happened?" I asked both boys gently.

Jonathan looked at Billy and then rubbed his shoes in the ground before speaking.

"We promised the guy we wouldn't say anything, but he swore he was a friend of yours and wanted to play a trick on you all. He seemed harmless enough. The two of us were together and I had my bat, so if he was a weirdo I was going to clock him one." Jonathan said.

Billy spoke up, telling me about the radio with the weird music and how the man had them each sneak up to either side of the gate, then turn on the radio and Jonathan went up and down the side of the house then sprinted to the other side and handed off the radio to Billy. From there Billy went up and down the sides then through the front gate and they met in the front and set the radio down by the door and then left. The man had given each boy twenty dollars for their trouble to do the prank.

I rubbed my chin as the pieces fell into place.

"Did you boys hide by the back of the property along the trees?" I inquired.

They nodded and Jonathan pointed at his sock.

"I got caught up by one of the trees and snagged my sock. My grandma hates when I do that," he said.

I looked at Billy's shirt. It was a San Francisco Giants baseball jersey. It was gray on black. I looked at the front and saw a small tear.

"Billy, did you accidentally run into the back step when you handed off the radio?" I asked him and looked into his face.

"Yeah," he said looking down. "It hurt but I didn't want to get caught. The man said to make sure that no one saw us," he explained.

I rubbed my chin thoughtfully and asked the final question.

"Did either one of you write anything on the dining room window?" I asked. Both boys looked at each other and shook their heads.

Jonathan interjected. "Heck, Mr. Royston, we're not tall enough," he said laughing.

I laughed with both boys, trying not to alarm either one of them.

"Do either of you remember what the gentleman looked like?" I asked.

Billy and Jonathan looked at me and shrugged.

"Not really now that you mention it," Billy said.

"All I remember was that he was wearing a funny hat," Jonathan told me. .

"He was wearing a long coat and he smiled and whistled that song that was on the radio," they both said.

A chill went up my back. I reached into my pocket to grab a business card and leaned down on my knees so I was down on their eye level.

"Do me a favor and let's keep this between us. Rhianna and Misty thought there were ghosts and you two scalawags pulled it off beautifully and gave them a bit of a fright! Next time, if you see our friend around, give me a ring, ok?" I asked, smiling and handing the boys my business card.

"I think the girls will want to pay back their friend and play a trick on him for today's hijinks," I said with a laugh. Billy and Jonathan both smiled and laughed with me.

"We thought we did something wrong," Billy said. I pulled at the bill of his baseball cap and smiled at him.

"No, you didn't do anything wrong; it was all in good fun. Now off with you both and not a word to anyone," I said smiling. Both boys nodded and took off along the fence line.

I rubbed my hand across my chin and made my way back toward Rhianna and Misty's house. If I told the ladies what had happened, it would only worry them more. I was going to have to have a private conversation with Detective Logan and see if maybe I could arrange for some extra protection or a patrol car in the area for a few days just in case. I would also confer with Reid and get his thoughts on the matter. As I looked up and down the street, the sun was now chasing the dusk and it was still very quiet. Hopefully, Reid and Logan had finished their interview.

I made my way back to the house with more questions rolling around in my head, but I did have answers. That was a start. The million dollar question being who had written *We All Fall Down* on the dining room window and unlocked the side gates? I rubbed my chin and made my way back into the house.

Chapter 2

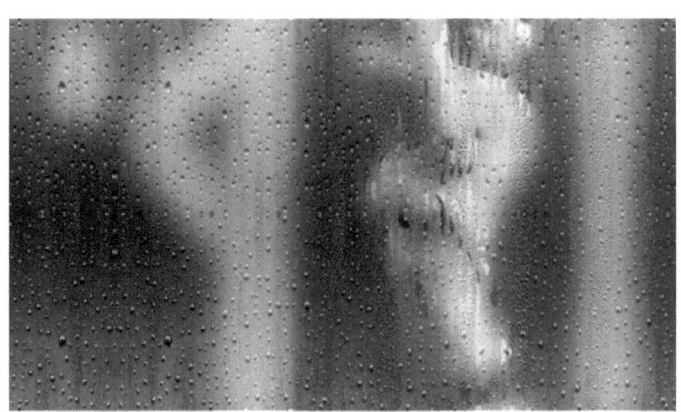

~Burnt Norton~

At the still point of the turning world. Neither flesh
nor fleshless;
Neither from nor towards; at the still point, there the
dance is,
But neither arrest nor movement. And do not call it
fixity,
Where past and future are gathered. Neither
movement from nor towards,
Neither ascent nor decline. Except for the point, the
still point,
There would be no dance, and there is only the dance.
I can only say, there we have been: but I cannot say
where.
And I cannot say, how long, for that is to place it in
time.
The inner freedom from the practical desire,
The release from action and suffering, release from
the inner

And the outer compulsion, yet surrounded
By a grace of sense, a white light still and moving,
Erhebung without motion, concentration
Without elimination, both a new world
And the old made explicit, understood
In the completion of its partial ecstasy,
The resolution of its partial horror.
Yet the enchainment of past and future
Woven in the weakness of the changing body,
Protects mankind from heaven and damnation,
which flesh cannot endure.

Excerpt from Four Quartets by T.S. Eliot

Rhianna~ I was glad to get the interview with Logan and Reid over with. My nerves felt as if they were being stretched a little too thin, and after the morning's freak show at my house, all I wanted to do was crawl in bed with Misty and take my mind off of things. Royston came walking in right as we wrapped up. We all looked up as he came through the front door. He had that thoughtful expression on his face, which was never a good thing. That look always meant he was thinking about something. I thought we had just about enough surprises for one day. Royston joined us at the table.

"How is the interview coming?" he asked. Logan and Reid both smiled.

"We actually just finished, old chap." Reid said.

Royston grinned at Reid, catching the small jab that he had thrown.

"Oh, you're a funny one for a yank. I suppose you think I go flying about San Francisco and clean chimneys with Mary Poppins, too," he replied, laughing.

At that point Logan and Reid both laughed and Misty and I joined in.

"Royston, If you get the straw hat and outfit and start dancing around with fucking penguins, you're totally going to lose your cred with the band man," I said laughing.

"Hey! Our chimney needs a bit of cleaning. Are

you feeling up to it?" Misty asked grinning.

Royston put both hands on his hips and tilted down his cap.

"Coming right up, Governor!" he said and grinned at Misty.

At that we all started rolling. God, I fucking loved him. He could take a punch and throw it just as fast, and he made fun of his own as much as he loved teasing us Yanks. It was a wonderful mix of the two, and he had a natural wit about him that made it easy to go along with.

I stood up from the table and stretched as my phone buzzed. I looked down and saw a picture of our friends down by the Embarcadero, smiling and hamming it up. The text message that followed was from Gia and it said:

"Are you done yet? Can we all go drink and play now?"

The next shot was of Abel and Elias. Fuck, the big gorilla wouldn't smile to save his soul. They had no idea what had happened at my house and I didn't want to be a buzz kill by telling them what had went down, at least not until Royston and the boys figured out what the fuck all the weirdness was. I looked at the guys.

"Are we all fucking done here? I think I want to grab a shot of Johnny Walker with Misty and take a nap,"

Logan and Reid both smiled and stood up.

"Yeah, we're done," Detective Logan said.

Logan handed Misty and Rhianna his card, and everyone shook hands as the guys headed for the front door. Royston whispered to me he would be right back and went with the guys out to their car. I was going to remind Royston to check on Laura and Ava later at the café. I still couldn't figure out what the deal was with the pie guy at the café and by the bridge. Misty slid her arm around me and played with my ass which brought a huge smile to my face. As soon as Royston was gone, I was going to get in an hour or more with her before meeting up with everyone downtown. Come to think of it, Chinatown sounded really good. Maybe we could head across the bridge and grab some dinner with everyone at Begoni Bistro. They were the new kids in town, but the food was outstanding. We had gone there on a spur of the moment type of thing, and sure enough, the food kicked ass.

Just the thought of Dim Sum, Peking duck, and cold beer made my mouth water. Misty's hand came down across my ass cheeks hard. I loved the sting. I looked over at my girl, smiling.

"Hey, you looked like you were daydreaming. Remember we have some business to finish up today before we go out with everyone later," she said grinning.

I was instantly wet as she rubbed my ass again. I wiggled it seductively, pulled her to me, and kissed her even though we heard the front door open. Royston came back in smiling. We separated for the time being until Royston was gone.

"What did you find out, Royston?" I asked, playfully crossing my arms.

"I asked Logan to send up a patrol car for a few days just in case anyone is lurking about. From what little we found outside, we don't have anything conclusive yet to go on, but rest assured, I'll work with Logan and Reid and see if we can get to the bottom of this. In the meantime, you have their number as well as mine, and most importantly, you still have your father's .38 just in case someone gets too nosy." He said reassuringly.

"Thanks, Royston. We're going to crash for a few. Do you and the rest of the band want to join us in Chinatown with everyone else in a couple of hours? I'm going to text Gia and tell her we will hook up with everyone for dinner because the interview went so long," I told him.

Royston smiled and nodded his head. He wasn't stupid; he probably figured we needed to unwind, but I didn't give a shit at that point. I was going to jump Misty hard and fast. I needed her and I knew she needed me just as badly. He gave us both a hug and told us to call if we needed anything or if we saw anything out of the ordinary, otherwise he would meet us in Chinatown later. We both blinked and he was out the front door like a shot. Misty ran over and threw the bolt. I went to the back door and locked both bottom and top locks. I rubbed my arms and looked at Misty.

"Let's pull the shades around the dining room. My nerves are still a little off," I admitted.

Misty smiled and we went to shut the blinds and make sure the house was secure all the way around. I grabbed her hand and pulled her into the bedroom. She looked at me seductively when I licked my lips. Fuck yes; this was going to be good. I opened our bedroom door and pulled her to the bed. Before she could move, I spun her around and grabbed her face, my lips meeting hers in one explosive motion of delight.

God, I had missed her, I thought to myself.

She met my kiss with equal fervor, her lips grinding against mine as my tongue darted forward parting her waiting lips. We slowly French kissed, my fingers moving skillfully over her clothing, unbuttoning and pulling, stripping her down with practiced ease. I could already feel the heat radiating from between her legs. The scent driving me over the edge as I dropped to my knees, my fingers sliding into the elastic, yanking her panties down in one quick motion as her legs parted. She was perfect in every way for me. I needed all of her. My face slid forward, my tongue hungry, darting and teasing her as she grabbed my head and spread her legs further. I could already taste her juices on my lips. She was soaked. I stood up and pushed her back onto the bed, my own need exploding. She watched as I ripped my own clothing off, tossing it everywhere. I slid between her legs and ordered her to grab the sheets and not let go no matter what.

My lips glided from the edge of her ankles up, and she opened her legs even wider. I looked down at her glistening beauty. The flower of her womanhood was opened, waiting. I teased and nipped, watching her quiver as I slowly worked my way up. She grabbed the bed and held on tight wanting to grab my head, but we had played this game before. She knew the reward was pure bliss. As I got closer, Misty began to undulate her hips, moaning seductively as I brought my fingers down, spanking her clit. She let out a gasp, knowing I wanted her to hold still. I lifted my head, smiling, meeting her gaze.

My tongue darted out, and I dove headlong into her waiting lips, teasing and sucking, nibbling along the edges, slowly swirling and parting as her moans rose and fell with my ministrations. The flavor that burst across my tongue was succulent and creamy, floral and mouthwatering. I drank like I had never tasted something so delicious. Bringing her to the edge then backing off. Her knuckles were white with how hard she gripped the sheets. I grabbed her legs and pushed them farther apart. Sliding two fingers in, I worked her, wanting to feel her full release against me. I felt the shudder run through her body as I started spiraling and increasing the tempo. As she moved her fists and pounded the bed, I could tell she wanted to grab my head. I moaned as I finally yelled from between her legs. "Now!" That was her permission to grab me.

Her hands locked into my blonde hair, pulling me

into her pussy as my tongue stiffened, penetrating her folds. She ground herself against my mouth as I met her thrusts while tasting her juices ran all over my mouth. Misty completely lost control, screaming as she held my head against her pussy, her hips bucking and moving faster and faster. I loved every minute of it. I needed her. I needed her release. I needed to hear her screams as my name started rolling past her lips. She was insane with lust as she held me tight, watching me pleasure her, giving everything to her lover.

My fingers moved in and out of her. Sliding a third finger in. she lost complete control. Her scream split the night as I felt a warm rush of fluid jet around my lips. I lapped hungrily, swallowing everything as she let go of my head. The waves of pleasure rocketed through her skin. I spanked her clit repeatedly as she came. Taking each orgasm, her body shuddered. Finally, she was spent.

I got up and padded to the bathroom, grabbing washcloths and towels. After I washed the traces of her orgasm from my face, I went to my lover and slowly cleaned her up. She shuddered; her pussy was so sensitive from my earlier touch. I tossed the towels into the hamper and lay down next to her, letting her arms wrap around my neck as she sighed contentedly.

"That was so unfair!" She exclaimed. "I thought I was going to take you first." I could feel her smile without even looking at her. I grinned.

"I needed to be in control for a minute. I didn't hear you complaining," I replied laughing.

"Fuck no, I wasn't complaining. You were determined to get every drop, honey," she said, grinding herself against my leg.

We both laughed. Misty leaned up on one arm and started teasing my nipples. I let out an appreciative moan. "Damn, I thought I had worn you out already, baby," I said and let out a small gasp.

"Oh, I'm tired alright, but fair is fair, Misty said and slid her leg between mine, flipping me on my back. She kissed me hungrily, her tongue sliding between my lips. I savored the moment, enjoying that kiss. It was passionate, hot, and most of all, it had a lot of heart. I loved making memories with her. She reached over to the nightstand and pulled out a small vibrator. She grinned at me and looked down.

"Hey, no fair! I went natural on you?" I said, causing my girl to laugh.

"Quit complaining. We still have to get Chinese food, but you're going to get rid of some of that stress. It's not up for discussion," she said matter-of-factly.

She slid between my legs, and I heard the hum as she turned the toy on. My whole body shuddered as she began using her talented lips and tongue on me. The toy was just an added bonus. The coup de grace so to speak. Misty knew my body better than any lover that I had ever had. She could make me climax with just the right look and touch. I surrendered myself to her and let her work her magic.

My own moans were soon slipping into the room

as she increased the tempo. My own fingers clutched the sheets as she gave the command, and I grabbed her head, grinding my wetness against her face, wanting her to take everything I had. I moved faster and faster, bending my legs and pumping against her as her tongue darted and explored. The toy moved as if it had a life of its own. She dialed it up one more level and that was it. I pin dotted as the orgasm washed through me. My back arched as I let go of her head and exploded all over her and the toy. I couldn't even speak after a moment it was so good. She wouldn't back off either; she kept pulling more and more out of me. I lost count of how many times I had climaxed before she finally stopped.

I remember sobbing even as she went to the bathroom to get towels and clean me. I just knew how I felt and at that moment everything was right in my world. She was gentle as I shook. We fell into each other's arms and just held each other. After a while we laid side by side, touching and exploring. I knew after dinner all bets were off. That was when we were going to really get down. As if on cue, our cell phones went off. We both laughed and grabbed our phones. Misty had pictures of Abel and Gia, and I had pictures of Elias and Genevieve. Our friends were waiting for us. I slapped her ass and told her to get a move on. Misty laughed and grabbed me and we both got up together.

"Let's catch a quick shower. Text them that we'll be right there," she said. I grabbed my phone and sent the message. She smiled from the bathroom as I followed her in. We wouldn't have time for another round, but foreplay could be just as fun as the actual act. Anticipation could do delicious things to your head, and mine was already planning our desert.

Chapter 3

~Burnt Norton~

Words move, music moves
Only in time; but that which is only living
Can only die. Words, after speech, reach
Into the silence. Only by the form, the pattern,
Can words or music reach
The stillness, as a Chinese jar still
Moves perpetually in its stillness.
Not the stillness of the violin, while the note lasts,
Not that only, but the co-existence,
Or say that the end precedes the beginning,
And the end and the beginning were always there
Before the beginning and after the end.
And all is always now. Words strain,
Crack and sometimes break, under the burden,
Under the tension, slip, slide, perish,
Will not stay still. Shrieking voices
Scolding, mocking, or merely chattering,

Always assail them.

Excerpt from Four Quartets by T.S. Elliot

Elias~ God, my head was still pounding from the party the night before. Royston really brought the party to Rhianna's house. I don't think I have ever eaten that much Mexican food or drank that much tequila and beer in one sitting. Well, that's bullshit. Let me rephrase that. Since I was in college with Abel is more accurate. It was one of those morning after wake-ups when you look around to see if you are at home or not and who's in your bed. When you finally roll out of bed to take a leak before staggering out of the bathroom, and you just stand there looking at the living room with your mouth open at the destruction everyone had wrought from the night before.

It was like a frat party on steroids, total Animal House. There were empties and food containers everywhere. I stepped out into the living room and could see the TV was paused on an old episode of Saturday Night Live. Speaking of Animal House, there was John Belushi on the flat screen dressed like Joe Cocker with the real Joe Cocker singing next to him. I had to laugh at the scene. I hit the play button on the remote and sat on the couch, watching the two of them go at it on stage. Those were some good times.

The house was still quiet, and everyone was still crashed. I walked into the guest room and found my Genevieve sleeping peacefully. There is something seductive, yet simple, in waking up someone you love with a kiss. The anticipation as you lean in and your lips brush across theirs. Realization from the sleeping party and the return pressure as their lips push back hungrily, then the soft moan and those beautiful blue eyes fluttering open, Fuck yes, it was perfect and just like that.

I leaned in and kissed her again and let it linger, letting her wrap her arms around my neck. There are no words to describe what it is like to lose someone you love. When I thought my brother Qaylin had taken her life, it was a feeling of utter desolation that ripped right through me and tore me open to the core.

It is a grieving that consumes all light like a black hole in the center of your universe. It pulls down at the edges of your soul, ripping and tearing grief that is all consuming. It is a pain that is completely indescribable and at times indecipherable.

My heart still raced when I touched her, felt her, and loved her. All the little things were amplified a million times more, and I held onto those moments like they were diamonds sitting in the palm of my hands. She was precious and she was mine. Nothing would come between us, and I would defend her with my last dying breath. I loved her completely. Looking into those beautiful eyes, I wanted to sit at a piano with her on top and just write beautiful music and pretend the world was not a shit storm and that we are not sitting right in the eye of the maelstrom. At that moment, she was a rock ballad waiting to happen, and I was the man that loved her. I don't know if that makes sense, but that was how I felt.

We all make mistakes and look back at those forks in the road when we realize we fucked up. There was no third time around for us, we'd both decided that. She wore my engagement ring proudly, and we would get to Paris to go see her folks soon enough to get their blessing. For now we had this time together and it was bliss. Genevieve just smiled at me and I returned it. Drinking her all in and crawling next to her in bed, we just laid there enjoying the moment, but reality, of course, comes knocking at the worst times.

My phone started buzzing as Genevieve started laughing.

"I would guess that is Abel calling?" she whispered and smiled at me.

Sure enough, it was a text message from Abel.

Hey, are you done camping at Rhianna's? You ready to hit the town? I am loading up the caravan and if your head isn't pounding like someone is slamming a double bass drum on your skull like mine, you will recall that Rhianna and Misty have to go meet those detectives for breakfast over at Ava's place anyways. Let's go fuck around man. The ladies will get a kick out of it and we can see what they added since the last time we were up here. I don't know about you man, but it's been a minute since I have been here except for touring and those don't count. We blow in and out so fast; fuck my manager is a prick sometimes!

I smiled and showed G the message. She started laughing and held her head.

I quickly typed in my response. *Yeah, we're getting ready. Give me a minute and we'll be right there. I'll have to redline the Vette since you're such an impatient fuck this morning!*

After a moment my phone chimed with his reply.

Ha ha asshole! We'll see you in a minute!

Fuck I loved him, he had a hair up his ass this morning, but he was right. We had time to kill. I checked on Rhianna and Misty and found their bedroom door open. They probably took their bikes and headed to Ava's. That's what I would do anyways. I pulled G out of bed and stripped her down quickly letting my eyes wander along the curves.

I pulled her to me and kissed her hard. She didn't bother resisting melting into my arms. My hand found her hair and pulled back as my tongue darted against her lips. She opened and met my assault full on, leaning backwards as I tugged then releasing as I wrapped her in my arms. We broke the embrace and I smiled at her.

"That was to let you know that I am going to have a lovely day with you and everyone, but the first chance that I have to keep you to myself, I plan on doing unspeakably sexy things to your body in the hopes that you will unintelligibly moan my name during the course of said events," I whispered to her.

The comment had her laughing as soon as I said it. She knew I was being playful even as I slowly started to reassert my control. I had to watch it, the doctors had told me it would take time and I had all the time in the world with this woman. We went and showered together. I kicked on the side jets and rain head and we both slid under the hot water. Genevieve stood still while I soaped her body and teased the hell out of her. Fuck, it was sexy as hell. I was enjoying the intimacy as my hands moved across her skin. Her nipples were rock hard and standing at attention from my ministrations with my cock following right behind. I wanted to take her hard in the shower, but we were fucked for time and we both knew it. As she turned around and started to rinse off, I brought my hand down firmly with a loud crack against her ass cheeks. She let out a yell and pushed her fists up against my chest and kissed me again under the running water. We broke the embrace and shut off the shower and dried quickly then headed into the bedroom. I slid on a pair of 501's and put on a black V-neck T-shirt and slid on a set of low cut boots and my pewter skull belt buckle to complete the look.

Genevieve slid on a matching black silk bra and panties set.

They were fucking delectable. I was going to tear those off later, and you better believe it. A set of denim jeans and black spaghetti strap top with the words Attitude emblazoned across the front completed the look. She looked hot and I loved every minute of it. We grabbed our leather jackets off the hat rack. My wallet was still in the pocket and Genevieve grabbed her purse as we headed out. We didn't have a key, but Rhianna would hook up with us later. We locked the door and found the Corvette waiting patiently in the driveway. I hit the remote FOB and started the engine and unlocked the doors. It was a nice car, not as nice as mine, but for a rental it fucking worked. We both jumped in and buckled up before I pulled out of the driveway and headed up the street. According to my bro he was literally right up the street.

Fuck me if we weren't there in like less than five minutes. When he said it was right up the street he wasn't kidding. He was already loaded up and waiting for us with his SUV running. I had to laugh, the prick. He wanted me to know that he was waiting on us and not the other way around. I pulled up alongside him, and he rolled the window down. Gia leaned over, waving at Genevieve. I knew Mia and Chance were in the back. Abel would not go anywhere without them. This was farther than five minutes so they came too. I liked seeing he was easing into family life. Nothing was easy for my buddy, but Gia was a perfect match for him. We didn't talk about it, but Mia had her daddy's heart in full lockdown. I hoped when G and I had our first child it would be the same way for us.

"Damn, that was the longest fucking five minutes of my life!" he exclaimed. I could see the shit eating grin on his face.

"Hey, you know how women are; they take forever to get ready. I was practically going out of my mind," I replied.

I felt a set of fingers pinch against the muscles in my chest. The move didn't escape Abel.

"Are you bullshitting me? Next time, I'll bring a

44

makeup artist from my tour along so we can have you ready on time," he said while laughing and waving us forward.

He pulled away from the curb, and I gunned the Corvette's engine and quickly shifted gears as we slid in behind him. Traffic was heavy, but it always is in the Bay Area. It doesn't matter what side of the bridge you're on. It seemed like it only took a few minutes until we were crossing the Golden Gate Bridge. The sunlight made the bridge pillars that much more brilliant. You could see across the whole bay. Cargo ships and freighters moved below us on the sparkling waters, the white wakes from their engines making white lines against the water as they churned forward toward the open sea.

Abel was headed toward the streetcar stations. We had talked about it the night before as the easiest way to get around the city. It was a smart move because parking was going to suck ass. Abel guided us over to Market Street where we finally found parking. We hopped out and locked up the cars as Abel got Chance and Mia together along with all of the things a young baby needs. I smiled at G, but made sure Abel didn't see me checking it all out. Gia caught me out of the corner of her eye but didn't say a word.

I bet she was thinking, *Yeah asshole you're next and then you'll see*, or something similar with lots of Gia attitude.

We headed over to a kiosk and bought day passes to the streetcars and before we knew it, we were headed up the Powell Mason line and straight toward Fisherman's Wharf. We ate and drank and made like tourists, we would stopping to send pictures to Rhianna and Misty. We even were able to get on the tour of the Rock in the middle of the harbor.

It was a great day full of clam chowder, Cioppino, clams and mussels, sourdough bread, and most of all, time with each other. Abel and I hadn't bonded like this in years. Maybe it was the years in-between or maybe it was that looking back at shit and realizing things were different now, but I knew one thing we were getting our friendship back and it really did feel like old times.

The girls window-shopped as we offered destinations to one another from our phones on different places that were must see. We rode the cable cars everywhere we went. We even went to the Cable Car Museum. About mid-afternoon, we sent a final set of pictures over to Rhianna and Misty. Rhianna told us they were done with their interview with the police and were getting ready to come out. They would meet us over in Chinatown for dinner. Abel and the girls seemed up for it, so we told them we would see them there and hopped back on the streetcar and headed toward Chinatown.

Fuck, that was a mistake. The girls went into a shopping frenzy, checking out new outfits for Mia. Abel shot down about half of them, but there were a couple that he couldn't say no to. I didn't say a word. I knew it was my turn next, and if I gave him shit; he would either punch me in the throat or mercilessly fuck with me until we started brawling. Friends and brothers are like that sometimes. We took our time walking through the shops and made our way toward Begoni Bistro. We walked up just as Rhianna and Misty were texting us and Royston slid in behind them.

"I have taken care of the reservations and our table is waiting," he said walking up to us.

I grabbed the front door and we slid inside to a very spacious and modern Chinese restaurant. The place was clean and the staff was very helpful. We were quickly seated and drink orders taken. The girls all ordered wine and the guys grabbed cold beers. We sat and took in the ambience as Rhianna explained the Dim Sum menu to us and recommended different dishes.

Everything looked fantastic, and we quickly waved the waiter over and started ordering Tapas to start and main courses to follow. You could see some of the dishes had a French influence but the overall main dishes were authentic. Everything that was brought to the table was absolutely delicious. Abel actually loosened up a bit for dinner and was as easy going as Abel could get, which wasn't a lot. I had to hand it to him though, since he was relaxed. Small plates were removed, main dishes slid onto the lazy Susan.

I think everyone was getting stuffed. Somehow we managed to plow through all the food and the waiting staff had egg tarts and Durian pastries ready to finish off any last vestiges of hunger that we had.

Coffee was served or tea if so desired.

It was a magnificent meal and a superb choice by Rhianna. Everyone was at ease, even Royston was telling us stories about growing up in England and where he got his start in the music business. He also mentioned the time he went to my parents place in Mesa to do some research on a Sherlock Holmes story he was working on.

Somehow he had learned that my family had quite an extensive collection of Sir Arthur's stuff, and he traced down the owners and contacted my family. I took a pull on my beer thinking of the irony of that. I was away at UCLA at the time, so I didn't know about it until years later when Royston was working with Rhianna and Misty and he told me the story. My old man remembered him and confirmed the story. What a small world we live in.

The plates were cleared and we were left with our drinks. The sun had already set. We were going to have to catch a ride back with Royston and the girls to the parking area. Abel got up to use the restroom, and I waved the waiter down to pay the bill. Before anyone could object I waved them to silence and handed the waiter my credit card. He quickly ran my card and brought us the bill. Abel came out of the bathroom as the waiter walked by him with a large smile on his face. I had of course given him a fat tip that was equal to the bill. I know I had made his night. Abel came walking up.

"What's with the waiter?" he asked.

"Nothing, I just picked up the check and gave him a fat tip. I figured you wouldn't mind," I said.

Abel looked at me and gave me the once over then the chin.

"Dude, you know I hate owing anyone a fucking thing. We always split the bill," he said. I could see his eyes were glowing so I moved quickly to defuse the situation.

"Abel, if you hadn't convinced me to come up here, we wouldn't be having the time of our lives. It's been way too long man, and it was my small way of saying thanks. Besides, bro, I had to fuck with you a little," I replied calmly.

Abel smiled and nodded and gave me that look that only he can. It was the look of ok, we are in front of company and our ladies, but next time I'll kick you in the balls prick look.

We left the restaurant with everyone relieved Abel hadn't gone short fused with asshole sprinkled all around. What I told him was the truth, I did want to say thank you to him and also to Misty and Rhianna and Royston. It was going to be great to pick up a guitar again. I was looking forward to our first practice.

We followed the girls and Royston to their vehicles and piled in and made our way back to Market Street. I was actually looking forward to some downtime with G after the day's events. I was tired but it was a good tired. G put her head on my shoulder as we dodged through the early evening traffic. I was looking forward to talking with Rhianna about what shows she had lined up, too.

She'd mentioned a few warm ups before the main event. I knew I was really fucking rusty. I'd be lucky if my fingers didn't cramp up when I started playing in Earnest again. That would be fucking embarrassing and I wasn't going to give Abel the satisfaction of signing like an old rocker past his prime. I needed to get some playing time in and the sooner the better. Maybe Rhianna could have the rest of her band come to her place and we could use the garage studio to do some freestyle jamming or something. My fingers were itching at the thought.

Royston dropped us off on Market Street by our car. We waited for Abel and the girls to join us. About a minute later, Rhianna pulled up and dropped off Abel, Gia, Chance and Mia. We gave everyone hugs and told the girls we would see them shortly. Rhianna asked Abel and Gia if they wanted to come over for a nightcap. They both actually yawned and passed saying they were going to crash at the rental and they would hook up with us tomorrow. I had a feeling Abel was going to do the same thing I was and wait till the coast was clear. It was supposed to be a relaxing vacation, and in my book, sex with a little domination was one of the best ways to relax.

Chapter 4

~Burnt Norton~

Time present and time past
Are both perhaps present in time future
And time future contained in time past.
If all time is eternally present
All time is unredeemable.
What might have been is an abstraction
Remaining a perpetual possibility
Only in a world of speculation.
What might have been and what has been
Point to one end, which is always present.
Footfalls echo in the memory
Down the passage which we did not take
Towards the door we never opened
Into the rose-garden. My words echo
Thus, in your mind. But to what purpose
Disturbing the dust on a bowl of rose-leaves
I do not know.

Excerpt from Four Quartets by T.S. Elliot

Rhianna~ It's funny what pops in your head over a cup of coffee. I was sitting with Misty in the living room reminiscing, contemplating what the next few days would bring. It was meditation for me. For all of the pretense, for all the rage, for all the anger I cast about and screams I ripped from the heavens. For all the stolen moments that had been taken from me, stripped from my soul I was in the end just me.

Rhianna Raines is what I gave to the world. The I image I projected of the badass bitch strutting on stage growling behind the microphone, pin wheeling my arms like the guitarist from The Who, and the screaming at the fans as we danced in a give and take of cause and effect was the most natural thing in the world. It was like waves lapping against my shore or a fist pounding against the door. It was years of honing my craft, kicking and screaming trying to make it to the top. There was a lot of pain as well. I guess that was why I was such a good storyteller and why I could weave dreams in my words and transport my fans to another world.

Sometimes, I took a brute force approach; I learned that from Abel Gunner. In your face, kick in the front door and blow them away, but other times I wanted to coax them into my world, into the music, into that moment of bliss where everything was perfect. The music, the crowd, everything flowing together seamlessly and we were communicating on a level that was spiritual.

I don't know if that makes sense to you, but to me music is sacred. It's my art; it is where I go to pray and speak to the chosen ones. I get what John Lennon meant about The Beatles and their popularity. It was like you were feeding the masses, feeding the five thousand. In my case I was shooting for sixty thousand or more, but Shadow and Flame had played to the five thousand. The gigs were getting bigger, the tickets selling out instantly. I was ready to move up, but I also knew from what the boys had taught me that as I moved up there was a blood sacrifice. I would sacrifice my personal life to the masses; the paparazzi were going to be more incessant, bigger assholes than they already were. Right now I was an up and coming, but once the wave crested and broke it would all change. I think my biggest fear was once I made it would I lose the woman that I was and change like so many others had and become what the people wanted?

It was a razor thin line. Many bands have tried it and lost themselves in the process. I didn't want to be a victim, pandering to the masses. Yet I wanted to make it. I wanted to stand in front of a quarter of a million people in my dream venue Rio and headline a concert where you couldn't hear yourself think from the noise of the crowd. Abel told me when he went to Rio that it was life altering. It had completely blown his concept of what a live gig was.

He said it was a fucking circus. There were so many people he couldn't see the horizon. It was just a moving ocean of bodies screaming and chanting his name. At that moment it was as close to God as a man could get and with it came power. The fans were everything; he lived for the moments with them. Gia and Mia owned his heart and soul, but when he stepped on stage and his fist slammed down across the strings, when he stepped up to the mike and started singing he went into another world. He told me I would understand what he meant once I got there, but I never forgot it. I wanted it, I breathed it, and I lived it. I wanted to make it that big.

The sun was rising over the bay; the fog had burnt off long ago. Royston had texted me that he was inbound with the band for some practice in the garage. He said that he had a friend of mine inquire if I would do a sit in for a few songs at a local bar. A quick slip in and out. I wondered who would pique his curiosity enough for him to ask me a favor like that. We hadn't really played bar gigs in quite a while. Once in a while we would do a quick in and out, but mostly we had graduated to bigger venues with marquees with our name splayed everywhere, so bar nights were few and far between. Royston was our manager and although I was the band leader, Royston took care of all the business aspects and honestly, he had been kicking ass doing it.

He had already texted Abel and Elias and asked them to join us. Abel didn't need the practice really, the man was a fucking beast on guitar and drove women ape shit mad with his music. Elias had some rust to knock off, so I'm sure that's why Royston wanted us to do a little tune up. He would be out of playing shape, sitting behind a desk and working out was one thing, but all of the little nuances of playing live could really take it out of you.

A car horn in the driveway broke my reverie. I went over to the front door and opened it up followed by Misty. The gang was all here and I was ready to lay down some music and see how it sounded. Heck if the boys were up for it, maybe we could record today. It couldn't hurt? I would ask Abel and Elias, maybe we could do a vault tape or something for later. I started laughing and Misty slipped her arm around my waste.

"What's so funny?" she asked.

"I was wondering if we could record today's session, but knowing Abel, I'm going to have to work on Gia to get him to do it," I said mischievously.

Misty laughed and nodded her head. She already knew that was the truth. Everything was calculated as far as Abel's career goes. He was a shrewd businessman when it came to the industry. He doesn't leave bootlegs lying about, if it's not his best, he doesn't necessarily want it out there for the masses. If it is live, the recording has to be top notch; it's his brand after all.

I got what he meant, back in the day though a lot of bands would release live albums consistently because the record labels believed it would keep the fans interested. I had a crap load of live records from back then. Mostly hard rock and metal but some old school jazz too. My grandma used to take me to the shows up at The Bowl and The Greek and we would slip backstage afterwards so I could ask the musicians to teach me their tricks. A lot of the legends thought I was a pretty far out kid. I also learned a lot about recording that way. They were tricks I brought into Shadow and Flame when we played live. As the years went by, I really honed our sound to a sharp keen edge. It was wholly our own, there were hints of other bands of other times, like it was classic but modern at the same time. I thought it was fucking perfect myself.

We walked out and greeted everyone. Abel had brought a guitar and so had Elias. My band already had their gear in the garage studio, and Misty's guitar was in a case in the garage so we were all set. Royston unloaded waters and coffee and set up a small table in the corner for everyone along with some pastries. It was what I loved about the guy, his attention to detail. He took good care of us and made sure that anyone visiting felt at ease. Gia, Chance and Mia went and sat in the recording booth with Royston so they didn't blow their ears out. Mia was playing on Gia's lap. Abel made himself right at home, grabbing a small Marshall stack. Misty grabbed the other one. Ace jumped on the drum kit and started warming up. Jezebel didn't miss a beat and slid next to Ace and plugged into the Fender Bassman and started getting warmed up.

I watched Elias out of the corner of my eye as he pulled his guitar out. He brought his black SG with him. He lovingly opened the case and pulled out his trusty axe. You could see the wear marks on the body and pick guard. He never did anything half-assed when he played. That guitar had been his friend for many years and it was good to see it out of the case again.

Royston had already arranged an extra Crate Stack for Elias. Elias opened another case and pulled out his effects pedals. All custom, built to tone his sound. He signaled Royston who made sure the channel was down when he plugged in and then gave him the thumbs up. Abel had a custom shop Fender Stratocaster with him. I loved the skulls that were painted on the neck; it was a nasty piece of red over black paint. The guitar was wicked.

He signaled Royston and popped open a case with his pedals as well. As soon as he plugged in, he tuned up; we all did at that point. I looked around at my band and friends. FUCK YES, I was ready. Abel and Elias both looked at me as I reached into my bra and pulled out the set list. I handed copies to everyone.

Abel whistled and looked over at Elias.

"Fuck yes! I haven't played some of these since I was touring with Insanity. You up for this cupcake?" he asked Elias fucking with him.

Elias response was to give Abel the finger and smile.

"You're an asshole, but I love you Abel," he replied and at that point we all laughed.

I raised my arm to signal Ace to count us in and that was when the magic happened. Music that had not been played live in years was suddenly flooding my studio space. We tore into old standards like "Skull Fuck" and "Give The Man The Finger."

Jezebel's bass thundered as the boys traded off rhythm and lead with Misty double filling on rhythm to really fatten the sound out. Kind of like what Def Leppard and Judas Priest used to do with twin guitars. It was a fat sound. I looked straight ahead as the girls were dancing in the control booth. It was ethereal the wall of sound and fury.

Both guys didn't miss a beat as they stepped forward alternating vocals and leads, letting me slide in for different verses and choruses. Elias hit a few bad chords and after we finished each song on the list he would go stand with Abel and review the notes and patterns until he had it right in his head.

Ace and Jezebel were both huge fans of Metal Insanity from back in the day, and since we played with them, they already knew the sound down pat. Abel didn't miss a beat as we tore into each song on the list. He was an animal pure and simple. It was great to see him in his element. My band was a well-oiled machine. Misty played with everyone, so if she got stuck on a part, she would ask Elias and Abel, but those moments were few and far between.

My girl knew her shit and she knew how to play. We encored with a song called "Submissive." It was one of Abel and Elias's early ballads, and a gem we pulled out from the archive for the show. Misty stepped up with me and we sang background harmony with Jezebel while the guys traded off lines. You would swear we had been a band playing with each other for years it sounded that fucking good. Royston gave us the thumbs up when we finished.

The girls were dancing around the sound booth with Baby Mia. We kicked ass and we were ready.

Royston stepped out and talked to us after. He said we would do one more walk through the day of the event and he asked Abel and Elias if they wanted to sneak in for a live concert we had at the Winery and possibly a small bar gig. Before Abel could say anything I told him the lowdown on the winery.

"Shit, that fucking sounds right up my alley!" he said gruffly. He looked over at Gia who nodded.

Elias was listening in as Genevieve walked up.

"Wine and kink? Sounds like a full on party all right! It will be like old times in LA Abel!" he said aloud.

Abel laughed, and we grabbed beers and headed into the house. Royston had already brought food in and had the dining room table setup with Italian pasta and bread, salad and wine. It was a great way to end the practice and we were all starving, but most of all we were all ready to do the show. The sound and feel was that good. The crowd was going to lose their shit when they heard us. I could taste it, feel it. Misty was as jacked up as I was. Even Royston was smiling. This was going to be big and if it went viral, well FUCK YES!

Chapter 5

~Little Gidding~

If you came this way,
Taking any route, starting from anywhere,
At any time or at any season,
It would always be the same: you would have to put
off
Sense and notion. You are not here to verify,
Instruct yourself, or inform curiosity
Or carry report. You are here to kneel
Where prayer has been valid. And prayer is more
Than an order of words, the conscious occupation
Of the praying mind, or the sound of the voice
praying.
And what the dead had no speech for, when living,
They can tell you, being dead: the communication
Of the dead is tongued with fire beyond the language
of the living.
Here, the intersection of the timeless moment.

Excerpt from Four Quartets by T.S. Elliot

Misty~ Fuck yes! That was fucking amazing. My head was still reeling from the practice session. We had torn into that set list with a fucking vengeance, and it was balls-out, kick-ass, and take fucking numbers good. I took a long pull on my beer. It was what we as musicians live for. I could hardly wait to get up on stage at the Fillmore; the fans were going to lose their shit. Abel and Elias sounded like they did back in the day. Yeah, Elias had to knock off some rust, but the fucker could still shred that SG like nobody's business. If Gia and Genevieve hadn't been in the sound room with Royston, I fucking bet we would have blown the curls right out of their hair.

Royston had the sound really dialed out and balanced. He was on his game like nobody's business. Jezebel's bass was thundering, and I thought I was playing next to Geezer for a minute the way she was rolling and slamming against the strings. When I looked over at her Peavey, I realized that she had restrung it with even thicker gauge strings. She really wanted the sound to be fat and damn it sounded killer. We had gone to see Sabbath and Heaven and Hell when they had toured through the area more than once. Royston always had pull and got us tickets and backstage passes. When it came to getting us tickets for gigs or getting us on the waiting list, Royston was the pimp. We never asked how he pulled it off, he just did.

Of course sometimes the bands would pull a fast one and have us slide onstage for an encore with them, but that was living the life. We weren't headlining, we were just enjoying the music and watching the metal gods do what they do and that is shred, take heads, and blow the fucking place up. I think my favorite times were drinking a cold beer with Tony from Sabbath and asking him if a particular story I had heard was true. The same with Ian, we got to see him with Purple. That was fucking epic. We all got trashed on tequila, and Royston being a smart ass actually rented a Rolls Royce to take us to the show. Being smart he got a regular Lincoln Town Car to take us home afterwards, I think he knew we were going to go all in with the partying that night. Those were good times.

I sauntered across the living room and wrapped my arms around my girl. Rhianna grabbed my hands as we partied with our friends. Elias and Abel were in an animated conversation, and I could tell they were talking about old times at UCLA. Gia and Genevieve interjected and laughed, and the baby was playing on Chances lap. It was nothing outrageous. In fact, if you took a picture, you'd find a bunch of laid back friends chilling and enjoying the moment.

I leaned in, letting my lips graze Rhianna's neck. She shivered. Yeah, we were going to have fun later. I smiled wickedly at the naughty thoughts flashing in my mind.

Jezz and Ace were chatting back and forth. Abel and Elias both heard them talking and barged into their conversation. Both of them laughed because it was a story about playing Club Kink in Los Angeles and they had been there. Jez rolled her eyes and gave me the middle finger just for shits and grins, and I smirked and returned the favor. I loved that girl, she was all attitude. Ace was asking Elias a question about drumming on a Metal Insanity track called "The Young Gods." Shit, that was an oldie; if I remember right, it was off of their first self-titled EP. Rhianna had a framed copy of it on the wall in the hallway.

"Who did the drumming on the track for that song?" he asked. The dude was fucking brilliant the way he did the rolls on the track and it sounded like a double bass drum. He was like really heavy on the playing. I must have listened to that song a million times when Rhianna first gave us the tape.

Elias gave Abel the look as he leaned forward and joined in.

"Fuck if I remember who did the playing on that track. Abel you remember?" Abel squinted his eyes and rubbed his chin.

"Fuck dude, that was a long time ago. Doesn't Rhianna still have that EP?" he asked.

I smacked my girl's ass and she reached to return the favor. I was of course too quick for her. She caught air as I dodged away.

"The guys are calling your name, beautiful," I said pointing. Rhi looked at the boys.

"You still got that EP from our first release?" Elias asked. Rhi smiled and walked into the hallway and came back holding a big framed picture. Abel covered his eyes.

"You still have that? Damn, if that ever got out Rhi There are some incriminating mother fucking paparazzi-worthy pictures there that I am not sure I want Gia to see," he growled, but I could see the smile on his face. Well as close to a smile as Abel would give.

As soon as he said it, Gia elbowed him and jumped up. Rhianna spun the frame around and everyone leaned forward. It was Metal Insanity. All vintage Polaroids of early shots, backstage and live. There was one picture called "The Golden Serpent" that raised some eyebrows.

Gia whistled as she looked over the pictures.

"I can see why you don't want anyone to see these," she smirked.

Rhianna laughed with everyone else.

"Yeah, this was when they pushed the leather look all the way. The fan girls ate it up and you know neither of them was shy, so all bets were off." She laughed looking at Abel.

"Right, Big Balls Tony!" she howled. Abel gave her a hard look and started laughing.

"You always thought that shit was funny. It was a costume malfunction, you little bitch," he said in a playful growl.

"Yes, so was the cobra picture," Rhianna replied

laughing.

Abel smirked and put his arm around Gia, looking at the pictures before pulling her back on the couch. Gia slid her leg over Abel's as she whispered something in his ear. Whatever it was she got a rise out of him.

Rhianna carefully opened up the frame and slid out the EP, handing it to Ace.

Ace smiled and took the album and flipped it around handing it delicately. They only made a few hundred copies. When they had first started, they couldn't give them away. Later they went into demand, but by then CD's and MP3's took over so the album versions were now highly sought after collector's items. Ace scanned the sleeve and liner notes before he found what he was looking for.

"So you guys did this at The Record Plant?" Ace asked. Abel snapped his fingers and nodded.

"Yeah that was it. According to this you just thanked a guy named Animal for drumming on the track. Who was that?" he asked.

Elias smacked his head as soon as he heard the name.

"You wouldn't believe me if I told you," he started laughing.

"It was Bonzo's kid!" he exclaimed. Abel started chuckling.

"Fuck, I forgot about that. He was in town with his band and we had hooked up at Slither and told him we were working on the EP. He was so trashed when he came in and drummed on the track. He asked us to keep it anonymous since he was under contract at the time with Geffen or one of the labels, the pricks," he said.

"No shit! No wonder. He has a distinct style of play just like his dad. The drumming makes total sense now," he said.

Just then my phone chimed with a text message. I looked down and saw it was Neely. I walked over to Royston who was sitting quietly in the dining room eating and showed him the text message.

"So you told Neely we would play at Reds?" I asked.

Royston laughed when he saw the message.

"I hadn't had a chance to ask you two. Since she is one of your friends and I do believe you're on good terms. She asked if we would come down to Reds and do a quick set, maybe an hour or so. She is trying to get more bands to book with them to pack the house. She took over their PR job," he said candidly.

"I don't know Royston, I mean we've drank there once or twice. It's more of a MC type of place, but we can hang with the best of them," I replied.

"Well, what I was thinking was we do a quick fan club announcement. You're playing Red's as Leather

& Lace or some such name to keep the place from getting mobbed and only fan club members that sign up will get in. Neely said she has a few guys to man the door and we can pack the place for her. You give your fans something intimate and personal, and we can do our tune up there," he replied.

"What about Abel and Elias?" I asked looking over at the boys.

"We don't want to let the cat out of the bag just yet. Let's see if they want to come along and just hang in the audience. If they do want to come up to play, they can, but if they just want to drink and enjoy the show, they can do that, too, and save the surprise for The Fillmore," he replied.

I waved Rhianna over from the living room and showed her the page.

"Royston, that place is a dive," she said.

"I did say we were going to play a bar, Rhianna remember?" he replied smiling.

Royston explained the plan, and Rhianna crossed her arms before waving everyone over. Ace and Jez were in immediately.

Abel laughed as soon as he heard the name.

"Fuck, I haven't heard that name in forever. Didn't we play or get drunk there when we were still in college?" he asked, looking over at Elias.

Elias started laughing.

"I remember Red. He is a shrewd business man, but he was fair. After he totaled our liquor bill against what he was going to pay us for the night, we owed him a hundred bucks!" he exclaimed.

We all rolled with laughter at the comment including Royston.

"Well, I guess we're playing Red's then," Misty held up her beer and everyone did the same.

Chapter 6

~East Coker~

You say I am repeating
Something I have said before. I shall say it again.
Shall I say it again? In order to arrive there,
To arrive where you are, to get from where you are
not,

You must go by a way wherein there is no ecstasy.
In order to arrive at what you do not know
You must go by a way which is the way of ignorance.
In order to possess what you do not possess
You must go by the way of dispossession.

Excerpt from Four Quartets by T.S. Elliot

Genevieve~ Attitude is everything in the music or fashion industry. Depending on your fans, you either strut out on stage and own the place or you go out with a quiet dignity and humility and the fans find it endearing. In the case of my mate Elias and his best friend Abel, the attitudes they have is kick the front door in and own the place. Pretty much the biggest meat in the locker room and get out of our way. Both of them have that element they bring to the party. It was one of the things that attracted me to Elias when we first met at UCLA. He walked in and he knew who he was and what he was about and he didn't back off of that position ever. When he hooked up with Abel and formed Metal Insanity, they cut their teeth at the local bars and venues in LA, but not once did they not know who they were or what they brought to the table.

Rhianna, Misty, and her band were schooled the same way. Go in and blow them away. Afterwards pick up the pieces and see who was standing. It was just a fact of life. It was good to see my future husband back in his element. Stripped of the suit and tie, stripped of the façade of corporate culture, he was back to just being the man I fell in love with. I liked it a fucking lot. The more we were away from Los Angeles and we both were away from all the responsibility, and just being with each other, just loving each other, just being in the moment, and fuck all the rest of it was an amazing feeling. Yes, Khyentse was in the background keeping watch on us. Yes, Elias was getting an occasional message about something he had to decide on, but for the most part the reality and the fantasy were almost separate, giving us time to really unwind.

Seeing him on the stage practicing, playing the hell out of that black SG, and the look of ferocious glee that was spread across his face warmed my heart. His head arched, shredding, jamming, going neck and neck with Abel. Fuck it was primal and I was wet as hell seeing him like that again. When we were in college after he was done playing, we would go back to his place and screw each other senseless. It was such a turn on watching him play, listening to the words and knowing which ballads were about me, about us. Fuck it was hot.

Gia and Mia and Chance were really digging the practice session as much as I was. It was free form anarchy in the sound booth. Royston was a good sport about it, considering we bumped and grinded him a couple of times. It was all in good fun, but yeah, it was good to have my Elias back again. Don't get me wrong, after all the shit that had gone down with his brother, I was grateful to still be walking and six feet up. We still had a shit storm to deal with at some point, but right now there was this moment, and we needed it desperately.

After the practice, I slipped easily next to him smiling. Cold beers and good Italian food always make for great times. Royston had impeccable taste,

I'll give him that. His sense of humor was well... English, but that was why the boys gave him a hard time. As soon as they asked about the gig at Red's, I started laughing.

Red's was a good bar; the owner was a pain in the ass. We hadn't played there in forever and a minute and that was being kind. If Neely wasn't asking, I wouldn't do it. Since she was doing the music promotion and helping Red out, I was ok with it. We would slide in the stage door, pack the place out, feed Rhianna and Abel's fans really quick and out we would go. I knew we could all hang backstage while the band jammed and I would get to see my baby in all his glory again. I was tingling just thinking about it. I hope Rhianna and Misty didn't mind me screaming later. I was going to be vocal after tonight's show that was a fact. I clenched thinking about it as everyone gave Royston the nod and we sat down to eat. There is something about Fresh Lasagna, Spaghetti and Meatballs, Eggplant Parmesan, fresh antipasto salad and bread. The whole meal was fucking fantastic. It was balls out delicious old school out of bounds good.

Ace and Jezebel went out to the garage and started staging gear on the driveway. I walked out with the boys as Royston slid around the side of the garage and fired up the band's tour bus that was under a canvas vehicle storage. Leave it to the British Pimp to score large for his girls. Everyone smiled when he backed out the black Turtle Top Vanterra XLT. It looked bad ass. Royston had pimped the shit out of the van with burgundy red and blue decals that matched Misty's hair with high resolution shots of the Golden Gate Bridge and Shadow and Flame's first album cover on it. There were also different live shots of the band performing on stage. Add opaque windows so you couldn't see inside from the outside and a divider in the back to stow the amps and stuff and a portable wet bar inside that was fully stocked to the nines and it was stylish.

Elias was a little distracted texting on his phone, I'm sure to let Khyentse know what the plan was and make sure there was extra security if needed. Abel walked around the bus and looked back at Royston.

"Fuck Royston, you scored on the wheels. No wonder the fans go ape shit when they see her coming into town," he said.

At that moment, it occurred to me going on the bus might be a bad idea for the small gig, I think Abel was thinking the same thing.

"Not a problem Abel, I'll take the gear down to the bar and unload with Jezebel and Ace and stash the van in a garage until show time. You all can take your own vehicles down instead. Besides it will throw any paparazzi that might get wind of the show off your trail. Does that sound agreeable to everyone?" Royston asked.

"I can see why Rhianna loves you. You think fast on

your feet. You're a regular cheetah sometimes Royston," Elias spoke up and chuckled, and then we all did.

Royston returned the smile. He knew they were fucking with him. It was his job to think of these things.

"I could rent a U-Haul and go completely non-descript, but the tour bus will get the fans going when they see it, it will be a nice precursor for The Fillmore," he replied with a quick smile.

Abel gave him the chin. That was his way of saying good thinking.

We all pitched in getting the bus loaded. We had the studio rolled up in no time. It totally felt old school at that moment, when we were first starting out. I knew I was in my head waxing all nostalgic, but things were a lot simpler then. Royston hopped in the bus with Jez and Ace and they headed to Reds. Rhianna and Misty left to join them and told us to hang out until tonight's show. Abel leaned over and whispered into Elias's ear. It had to have been something nasty because Elias started laughing his ass off. Abel looked over at me.

"I'm going back to the rental to kick with the missus and baby. We'll hook up with you later at Red's," Abel said smirking.

Elias couldn't resist the comeback and leaned over and whispered in his ear.

"You look like you're going to bang the shit out of Gia and don't even tell me that is not what you have planned you fucker," he told him.

Abel started rolling with laughter and Gia raised her eyebrows. Elias leaned over and whispered in Gia's ear what he had said. She tilted her glasses down and fist bumped him.

"You're damn fucking right that's what's going to happen," she said back and flipped her glasses down.

Abel wrapped his arms around Gia and grabbed her ass pulling her close.

"Catch ya," he said. They all walked to their car while I grabbed Elias and pulled him into the house. Gia wasn't the only one that was about to get hammered and I was going to enjoy every fucking inch of it.

Chapter 7

~*Burnt Norton*~

Here is a place of disaffection
Time before and time after
In a dim light: either daylight
Investing form with lucid stillness
Turning shadow into transient beauty
With slow rotation suggesting permanence
Nor darkness to purify the soul
Emptying the sensual with deprivation
Cleansing affection from the temporal.
Neither plenitude nor vacancy. Only a flicker
Over the strained time-ridden faces
Distracted from distraction by distraction
Filled with fancies and empty of meaning
Tumid apathy with no concentration
Men and bits of paper, whirled by the cold wind
That blows before and after time,

Excerpt from Four Quartets by T.S. Elliot

Rhianna~ It was great to see Neely. It had been a minute since we had talked. She was waiting for us behind the bar when we pulled up already going over things with Royston. She was efficient, I'll give her that. Ace and Jezebel were already unloading and moving our gear into the bar. Red slid out the back door when he saw us pull up and walked up and shook our hands and thanked us for coming down. He still looked the same, grizzled and hardened, a no nonsense type of man that didn't take anyone's shit. He was a shrewd business man and was a tough negotiator. Royston always had his hands full with him, but in this particular case we were doing Neely a favor, so Red was covering grub and drinks as long as we didn't abuse the privilege.

We walked up to Neely and gave her a hug. Neely kept thanking us repeatedly for coming. When Royston told her who else was joining us for the set, her eyes got really big.

"Shit, I'll make sure that Tommy and John are working the doors and I'll put extra guys on the back to make sure no one sneaks in," she said.

She leaned over and whispered in Red's ear and told him what was up.

"Abel and Elias? That was that band out of LA, Insanity something or other. I remember those two. Damn near emptied the bar one night. I thought they were going to start a fight when I told them they owed me money after playing for me. The bar bill was through the roof!" he exclaimed.

We all laughed when we heard the story. There had been some years between the last time they had played Red's and now and Red was happy they were going to stop in during the set. Since he wasn't paying us the house minimum, he didn't mind bringing in extra guys to cover in case the fans get rowdy.

Misty and I jumped in and helped everyone get the stage setup. Neely told us she would have one of the guys keep an eye on our gear until show time. We went up to the bar and Red handed everyone cold beers. The place was quiet. Usually Red would get a lot of MC types in, but today the jukebox was playing and just a few of the locals were hanging at the bar, shooting darts or playing pinball. Neely sat to the right of me and started talking my ear off.

"Misty came in for a quick visit awhile back, I was going through a rough breakup and needed an ear. I keep telling her to drag your happy ass over here, but you're always busy," she said.

"We both are. She's back and forth to LA a lot and I'm working on new album material in the studio with Royston and taking care of things, you know how it is," I told her.

We chatted back and forth while Royston went and stashed the bus. He went over and checked the sound board. Jez and Ace were running a sound check and making sure we were ready to go. The acoustics would change once the place was packed, but at least we could get our preliminary stuff done. Royston was a wizard about dialing in our sound during live gigs. Red's didn't have the best sound setup but he would push it hard and with Abel and Elias playing they were going to need it.

Neely reminded Royston there were some older speaker cabinets in the back. They hadn't had any headliners in a while, so they weren't used much, but if he wanted to add them to fatten out the sound he was more than welcome to grab them. Royston followed her pointed finger and found the cabinets. They were older Cerwin Vega's but Jez would love what it did for her bottom end sound, so would Ace. We all pitched in and moved them into place. It was just like old times, and I could see Misty grinning too. Tonight's show was going to be a great warm up.

We stepped onto the stage and I plugged in. Misty worked the board while I did a few vocal checks. Everything sounded good. Neely dropped the drapes so our gear and the backstage area were cut off. We ordered some burgers and fries and everyone hung out until the boys got there.

Royston went out to check something with the sound man and when he came back, he had a big shit-eating grin on his face.

"I dropped the bomb on the fan page that you were doing an impromptu gig at Red's with a few special guests," he said.

"So, what happened?" I asked already knowing the answer.

"Let's hope Red has enough security. I might have to call for additional bodies to work the front of the stage once the fans realize who is playing with you," he said.

Neely walked over, overhearing the conversation.

"I can get four more guys to work the front if we need it. I know you guys are a big draw and Abel Gunner...Holy Fuck! The place is going to go postal!" she exclaimed.

"Your damn fucking right the place is going to go postal! Abel and Elias are going to blow the roof off of the place. We're going to play so loud and shred so hard, we're going to blow the curls right out of your hair," came a voice from behind me.

We all turned as Elias and Genevieve walked in with Abel, Gia, Mia and Chance following.

Neely clapped her hands and ran over to greet everyone.

Abel and Elias both fist bumped Neely. Neely cooed over Gia & baby Mia, who she hadn't met yet. While the boys brought in their guitars and effects pedals and got them plugged in and setup, us girls talked and as long as Gia, Abel, and Chance were ok with it, we took turns playing with baby Mia.

Neely's phone buzzed with an incoming text message and she glanced down to read it.

She laughed.

"Red might need some help. He just texted that the place is filling up quick. I called Deena and Kathy in to help work the tables just in case. It's going to be a good night," she said, relaying his message to us.

"Looks like you made Red happy," she said.

The boys both nodded.

"Tell him we will go easy on our bar bill tonight," Abel replied. We all started laughing.

We could hear the cat calls from the other side of the curtain. Neely had one of the guards bring her a two-way radio so she could keep tabs on things.

"When the show is over, I'll have you pull your bus in the back to load up. The guys will make sure the fans are kept at bay unless you want to meet and greet with them. If they're off the chains crazy especially after seeing those two; that will probably be a bad idea. Just let me know how you want to play it," she said. She gestured at Abel and Elias.

"What? We're just a couple of guys jamming with our friends," Elias quipped.

Neely gave Elias the finger and laughed.

"Yeah, yeah, I remember how the girls latched onto your nuts, both of you," she said laughing. Gia gave her a look which Neely caught.

"No disrespect intended Gia that was just how shit went down back in the day," she said.

Gia laughed. "I was going to say, I'll cut a bitch that grabs Abel," she replied.

I knew Gia wasn't kidding. We all did. Genevieve smiled wickedly and fist bumped Gia. The boys were well protected.

The security radio chirped. Neely listened holding it close to her ear. Royston had already taped the set list down in front of where everyone was playing. I gave Neely a copy.

"Fuck yes! This is going to be epic," she said while looking at the list.

"Go ahead and drop the lights. You all ready?" she asked.

Abel growled, "Let's do this!"

We nodded and took our places.

The crowd was screaming at the top of their lungs. Royston signaled and opened the curtain. We were greeted by a wall of sound as Abel and Elias walked up to the microphones and yelled in unison. The fans were stunned. People were pointing, recognizing Abel immediately. The place erupted as the lights flashed and both boys slammed their hands down across the strings and launched into "In your face." Ace and Jez locked in tight with them as the song blew off the stage. People were jumping up and down pointing at Elias. It had all come together. Metal Insanity was together again. The crowd had no idea, and Royston had us dialed in perfect. It was loud and proud and pure adrenaline rush as the boys traded vocal lines

"In your face,

That's what we are,

In your face."

Abel went vertical his guitar, screaming the chords thundering as Ace slammed into the drum kit and Jez's bass tied in. I was singing harmony with both as I screamed across both of them. The sound was primal, and the crowd was losing their shit as we wrapped it. I walked up to the microphone and introduced myself and asked how everyone was doing. You would swear there were thousands in the place. Red's was packed to capacity. There were people looking into the windows wanting in.

Neely brought in the reinforcements while I introduced Abel and Elias and maybe, mentioned Metal Insanity. I couldn't hear myself think. People were beside themselves as Abel growled and launched into "Chains" and "Buzz Saw Bitch." We tore through the set with a vengeance, interchanging

Shadow and Flame tracks with Metal Insanity. It was perfect. Elias and Abel couldn't stop smiling. Elias found his playing chops and was tearing into his SG like an animal. Misty was tastefully mixing in leads and rhythm, and I played on one ballad "The Oceans Song" that Neely had requested.

We encored with "Catastrophe" and "Balls Out" and dropped the curtain. The fans were jumping up and down shaking the whole bar. Royston was already out the back grabbing the bus, and Neely was on the radio making sure the alley was blocked so we could load out. Royston grabbed us and told us to head out with Elias and Abel and to take Jez and Ace with us. The fans were still screaming as we grabbed our guitars and tossed them into the back of the SUV.

Abel and Elias stashed their guitars and quickly, jumped in their cars and hauled ass out of there. I checked with Royston to make sure he was ok. He gave us the thumbs up as Neely and her guys helped him load out our stage gear. We had just given the fans a taste of the show, and the reaction was off the chains. I felt like Misty had just screwed the shit out of me I was so elated. I could see the adrenaline rush on everyone's face. I texted the boys, and we all decided to meet back at my place afterwards. I texted Royston the plan and he sent me back the thumbs up signal. I leaned back in the seat and closed my eyes for a second. Misty was driving and she deftly wove us in and out of traffic. I just wanted a cold beer and to go another round with Misty.

I grabbed her thigh as we were driving. She moved her hips as I rubbed my fingers across the outline of her crotch, teasing her. She bit her tongue and looked over at me. Icing on the mother fucking cake…

Chapter 8

~East Coker~

*I said to my soul, be still, and wait without hope
For hope would be hope for the wrong thing; wait
without love,
For love would be love of the wrong thing; there is
yet faith
But the faith and the love and the hope are all in the
waiting.
Wait without thought, for you are not ready for
thought:
So the darkness shall be the light, and the stillness the*

dancing.
Whisper of running streams, and winter lightning.
The wild thyme unseen and the wild strawberry,
The laughter in the garden, echoed ecstasy
Not lost, but requiring, pointing to the agony
Of death and birth.

Excerpt from Four Quartets by T.S. Elliot

Misty~ My whole body was shaking from pure adrenaline. I felt like I had just railed a line of speed. My heart and brain were running at full tilt as my foot pressed the accelerator on our SUV and we made a beeline out of Reds. The show had gone off beautifully; I mean there were no fucking words to describe what had just happened. It was like we had blown the doors off of the place. It was a total rock and roll moment and it was Fuck Yes! I didn't know what else to say.

Having Rhianna playing with my pussy while I was driving was only amplifying the pleasure I felt from playing a kick ass show. I knew Rhi could feel how hot I was getting from her actions. I wanted her to unzip my jeans and grab me. I undid my belt and let it fall apart so she could undo the top button of my jeans. Fuck they were tight. I reached down pulling a few more buttons loose so she could reach in and dial me up all the way. She wiggled her hand in and found me soaking wet. I didn't care. I wanted her to see how worked up I was. She stroked, letting her fingers glide in and out with practiced ease. My moan rolled easily off of my lips as I continued driving. She kept her eyes on the road with me in case I got a little too carried away. Thankfully, traffic wasn't too insane as I let her tease me, sliding her fingers out; she stared at me and smiled taking her wet fingers and sucking my juices. I trembled at the sound.

"You are driving me fuck nuts, crazy baby. You are so in for it later." I licked my lips.

She slid her fingers back in as we crossed the bridge, pulling on my nub and really getting me hot. I bit my lip and moaned loudly.

"No Fair! You know I can't return the favor," I responded.

Rhianna leaned over and nibbled on my ear teasing the shit out of me. I swerved and she grabbed the wheel. I regained control and she laughed sliding her fingers out again and sliding them into my mouth.

"What's wrong, baby? You know if you're this wet, I am just as soaked," she whispered as I licked my juice from her fingers, sucking on them delicately.

I shot my hand between her legs and could feel the heat. She was just as ready as I was. We were going to have to keep the celebration short tonight; I was going to fuck the hell out of her later. That sounded crass even in my own head, but I continued to rub Rhianna through her jeans as we turned onto our street and headed to our house.

Luckily, Jezebel and Ace had ridden with Elias and Genevieve. I loved my band mates, don't get me wrong, but I loved a little foreplay with Rhianna in public even more. We had engaged in public sex in the past; it was one of my kinks.

The thought of getting caught was absolutely delicious. What can I say? I can be a real nasty girl at times. It comes with the territory. It was one of the things we enjoyed about each other - the exploration and pushing each other sexually. Tonight was going to be no holds barred. I hope Elias and G didn't mind the noise.

I hit the garage door opener and pulled in with practiced ease. I quickly turned off the car and stepped out and around the front of the SUV before everyone else pulled up so I could put myself back together again. Rhianna exited the passenger door and smiled wickedly as I buttoned up.

I hit the close button on the door and nothing happened. I turned around and hit the button again. The door lurched and went down partially then back up again.

"Honey, the garage door is acting weird again. You want to give me a hand? Maybe Royston can look at it when he gets here," I suggested.

Rhianna came around to me and we walked over to the garage door sensor. There was no fog this time, just a clear night in San Francisco. We looked up the driveway as our friends came pulling up.

"What the fuck is wrong with this piece of shit?" Rhianna exclaimed.

"Honey, did you hit the sensor with the trash can or anything?" she asked.

"Not that I know of, baby, why?" I asked.

"The reflector thing is bent," she said.

Rhianna bent down and straightened it out with her hand and asked for me to go try it again. I hit the button and the garage door lurched and started to come down. She broke the beam accidently and it stopped and lifted up again. Abel and Elias walked in through the garage followed by the girls and band. Rhianna let out a yell and everyone smiled and pumped their fists as she led them into the house.

I studied the reflector. What was weird was that it was bent was on the opposite side of where we took out the trash. Who knows? Maybe Royston bumped it when he was cleaning up the other night and jiggled it loose. My nerves were still a little frayed from the weirdness yesterday.

I hit the garage door button and looked out onto the drive as it was closing.

What was that? I peered out and thought I saw someone wearing a hat at the end of the driveway. I knew Royston would be along in a minute with the bus, so I hit the button again and grabbed a golf club. I carefully walked out, but I didn't see anyone. I knew if I screamed the boys would be out in a hot second to kick ass, but that was strange? Maybe my eyes were playing tricks on me. I closed the garage door and made sure it went down all the way. I checked the side door to the garage and made sure the locks were set. Satisfied, I went back into the house and joined everyone.

Abel and Elias were talking animatedly while Jez and Ace were talking with Rhianna. Everyone was still jacked up from the gig. Gia and Chance were talking to Genevieve, who was balancing Mia on one hip. It was fucking awesome. I slid in and grabbed a cold beer out of the fridge, seeing headlights flash on one of the side windows.

I told Rhianna Royston had arrived and went to meet him. Jez and Ace joined me to greet our manager. I grabbed a Boddington's Pub Ale out of the fridge; I knew Royston loved that fucking beer. He pulled in and dropped the canvas cover and joined us. I handed him the beer as we all threw our arms around him.

Royston laughed and joined us in our revelry, cracking the can of beer open and heading into the house with us.

I stopped him. "Do we need to offload? I thought I saw someone standing at the end of the driveway. Did you see anyone when you pulled up?" I asked.

"I didn't see anyone, but not to worry, love, since we're playing again tomorrow. Derek called me about that Winery gig for Forest. You remember the one for human trafficking with the um, special playroom?"

I covered my mouth and started laughing. Jez and Ace both looked at us.

"What wine gig?" they asked.

Royston turned and filled them in and everyone started laughing when he relayed the catholic school girl and nun outfit comments that Rhianna and I had made! Jez being a good sport really started getting into it.

"Shit, the women should dress like school girls, and we can have the boys dress like priests!" she said laughing.

At that, we all burst out laughing. Given half a chance I bet I could get Royston to go along and get the outfits. I remembered the place was a private winery in Napa, so the whole outfit thing would be tacky since it was a benefit show. I was curious about the dungeon. I didn't know if Rhi would be up for that particular form of kink, but maybe we could get Forest to give us a tour after the show. From what Derek had said we were playing with Angel Fire and Beneath The Burn. Both bands were red-hot and tearing up the billboard national and international charts. After tonight's gig, we could hold our own with anyone.

"Did you tell Rhianna the gig was tomorrow, Royston?" I asked.

"Forest just texted me and Derek. We already said yes and there will be some rather well connected people in attendance. They said the crowd will only be a few hundred. Think of it as a command performance for the president, my dear," he replied.

We walked into the house. Royston leaned over and showed Rhianna the text message. Rhianna put her fingers between her lips and whistled, startling everyone. Mia laughed when she heard it.

"Hey, Royston just reminded me that tomorrow's the gig for Forest down in Napa! It's a catered event at a private vineyard. Elias and Abel you want to come hang?" she asked.

Abel and Elias looked at the ladies and waited for the nod. When the nods came they both gave Rhianna the thumbs up.

"This might be a little bit of a reserved crowd. Maybe we can go over the set list and do a Shadow and Flame set and encore with Metal Insanity. That way you all can relax and soak up the atmosphere" she suggested, smiling sweetly at us.

"Oh my God, you are so full of shit!" Abel exclaimed.

We all burst into laughter.

"What I think she meant, Abel, was that it was going to be a suit and tie kind of crowd, maybe you whipping your dragon tattooed cock out to the masses might be a little over the top," Elias responded.

Abel growled, grabbing Gia and gave Elias the stink eye.

"Abel, I'm kidding. You know our dads both come from money. This is a charity gig the girls got invited to as Shadow and Flame, but we can go back them and encore with a few of ours. I'll donate some cash to the cause. If you want to chip in that would be fucking awesome, brother. What is the cause anyway?" Elias asked.

"Forest, the host, is raising money for the prevention of human sex trafficking." Royston interjected.

Abel raised an eye.

"I'll toss in some coin. Is there anything else I need to know about this gig?" he asked.

Royston smiled before Rhianna cut him off.

"From what Derek told us, our host, Forest, is not only a local wine grower and producer, but he has a special area of the house called The Cellar for his guests that like to partake in certain forms of kink" she informed everyone.

Abel palmed his face and looked at Royston.

"Dude, you're the only motherfucker I know that would book a gig for the girls at a party like that!" he said laughing.

"It is for charity!" Royston reminded him.

We all continued talking animatedly before everyone started getting tired. Jez and Ace both gave us the sign they were hitting the road. Mia was fussing even with Chance and Gia pulling tag team duty.

The party broke up pretty quick. Abel grumbled he would see us tomorrow sometime as we fist bumped and hugged. Elias and G started to help cleaning up the empties and snacks, but Rhianna and Royston waved them off.

"Sleep tight you two. Hopefully, we don't keep you up." Rhianna let slip.

Genevieve leaned over and whispered into Rhianna's ear, and both girls started laughing. Elias walked across the living room and beckoned Genevieve to join him. She padded over, taking his hand, and they made their way to the spare room.

"What did she tell you?" I asked playfully.

Rhianna leaned over and whispered in my ear, "I can't tell you how much this trip has meant to us. I hope your girl gives you a good workout in bed tonight."

I laughed and shook my head as Royston helped us clean up.

"Would you two mind if I use the spare room in the loft above the garage? After your comment about someone at the end of the driveway, I think it best that I be close by in case something happens," he explained politely. Rhianna smiled and gave him a hug.

"Here, let me grab fresh linens. I'll sleep better knowing you and Elias are here. That was some freaky shit yesterday, and I still don't know what it all meant. By the way, we should check on Laura and Ava tomorrow. Maybe we can go to the café and get some breakfast before we head up to Napa for the gig." she requested.

"Let's play it by ear. We want to get on the road early enough that we can take our time. We don't want to be pressed, especially with that crowd," Royston replied.

Rhianna handed Royston towels and linens.

"I bet you have an overnight bag in the boot of your Mini Cooper too, right?" she asked. Royston grinned and I gave him a hug.

"Don't think for a minute we don't love you for that. Thanks for staying tonight," I told him.

Royston gave us the two-fingered salute and walked up the stairs to the bedroom over the garage. I grabbed Rhianna and pulled her with me into the bedroom.

"Whoa! Shower then you can have it all, honey," she replied.

I closed the bedroom door and locked it, turning to find Rhianna's arms up in the air as if to grab me. She lowered her arms down by her sides. I loved the way her blonde hair cascaded over her shoulders. I pulled it aside and kissed her. I slid my hands along the side of her face and pulled her into me, letting my hungry lips press against hers. Her tongue danced against mine, and I needed to feel her skin. I brushed my fingertips along her jaws, down her neck, until they reached the top of her blouse. I had one button loose when she pushed my hands away. Breaking our kiss, she pulled the shirt over her head. Her breasts were held in place by a black lace bra. I reached up but she had already undone the clasp in the middle, allowing the bra to spring open. My hands cupped both, my thumbs teasing her nipples as I kissed her lips and neck, tracing my way down. She inhaled sharply as my mouth teased and bit her nipples. She held still while I undid her belt and pants. She sat on the bed as I pulled her boots off, grabbing the bottom of her jeans in the process. I yanked them down leaving her in a small pair of black silk panties and socks. Fuck she was hot. I kissed and sucked the inside of her legs as I slowly crawled up her body.

"Hot shower, remember?" she asked, tapping my shoulder.

I laughed and stood up, and Rhianna didn't waste any time stripping me down with the same practiced ease. I dropped to my knees, pulling down her panties as I went, and then helped her with her socks as she with mine. We kissed and teased each other as we made our way into the shower.

I reached in and turned on the rain head. We stepped in, letting the water wash over our skin and hair. I turned her around and soaped her hair. I gently kissed her neck then washed and scrubbed her soft skin. She smiled while returning the favor. I loved shower sex. You could get as nasty as you wanted and wash away all of your sins afterwards. We continued to clean and tease each other like crazy which just heightened the excitement. I had her grab the edge of the walls while I rinsed her off, bringing both hands down firmly across her ass cheeks with a loud crack. Rhianna let out a yell and rubbed her ass, trying to lessen the sting before she returned the favor. Her hand dealt quick slaps to each of my cheeks, and it was delicious. It was the best kind of foreplay.

Rhianna shut off the water after we both rinsed, and we grabbed large Egyptian cotton towels and carefully dried each other off. She took my breath away every time. I loved the peeks of her skin as my fingers worked over her body, drying carefully. It was intimate and something we did for each other. It was like an act of reverence. We loved spoiling each other sexually and especially with the small gestures of affection. What many couples don't realize is those small things, when you show someone you really care and love them, they add up.

I led her into the bedroom and pushed her onto the bed. We slipped into our embrace, kissing and exploring, teasing and biting. Each element fused into the next. She flipped me onto my back, her hungry mouth finding my heat. I slapped her ass and pulled her over my mouth, letting her slowly lower herself onto my waiting tongue. God she was delicious. I could taste her juices running out as I hungrily lapped and explored all of her. Her fingers slid down, opening me delicately before hungrily taking and driving me even higher.

We both sighed and moaned contentedly. Knowing my girl, I knew she wanted more as well. I broke from our embrace and crawled over to the edge of the bed and opened the drawer in the nightstand. I reached inside and pulled out a small velvet bag that had our special toys in it. Rhianna smiled as I glanced back at her over my shoulder, and she crawled on top of me, grinding herself against me. We both needed more, so I gently pushed back against her.

"Easy, baby, were both going to enjoy this," I said.

I grabbed her ankle and flipped her onto her back then reached into the bag and removed a beautiful black double-sided dildo with the controls right in the center for both parties. Rhianna moaned at the site of it, and I ran my tongue over my lips. My pussy was aching to be filled, and this toy along with the added accessories I had purchased were going to leave us both wrecked.

I reached back inside the bag and pulled out the lube. We were both soaked, but this toy wasn't small, and when it was dialed up, we wouldn't want any slip ups. Literally. I carefully worked the toy back and forth, sliding it in gently. Rhi gasped and moaned as I worked the shaft in about halfway; careful not to flip it on. She shook as I attached the padded restraints that would link both of us together. I slid them under her ass and thighs and clipped the front before putting the harness on. Once I was ready, I slid my leg under hers and lubed the other side of the toy, working my pussy down the shaft deeper and deeper with my motions pushing against Rhi. She was moaning and thrashing as the vibrator slid in and out of her with my movements.

Oh my god it felt good! As I got closer to her, I clipped us together. Now we could both ride without the fear of the dildo slipping out of either of us. I reached between us and flipped the switch, sending waves of pleasure through our bodies as the vibrator became alive inside of us both. The pulses were intense as we pushed against the other, taking more and more of the fake cock into ourselves.

I reached out and found her hands and pulled her closer as we matched thrusts. Rhi was shaking and my pussy was going crazy. I thrashed, pounding harder and harder into her. Rhi reached down and hit the dial, sending us both over the edge simultaneously. We went faster and faster and quiet was out the door as we both moaned and became very vocal. She gripped my hands tightly as my orgasm matched hers, and we both started coming, driving the toy deeper and deeper into us.

I couldn't even speak it was so intense. We were both spasming as waves of pleasure washed through us over and over again. I reached down somehow and hit the switch, and we both came again as the vibrator went to the highest setting. Neither of us could escape because of the harness. Rhi pushed against me screaming as I thrashed. My pussy was exploding. We both came so many times we lost count. Rhi grabbed the button and shut it down.

The bed was completely destroyed. My cum glistened on her skin. I had come so hard I squirted my release. Rhi smiled looking at me. That was when I felt the wetness all over my thighs and legs. My beautiful baby had matched me perfectly. Slowly we grabbed each other's arms and pulled ourselves tight and undid the harness. We slid apart letting the toy out slowly. Both of us were extremely sensitive. We only used the "black raven" on certain occasions, and we were always completely exhausted after a session.

Rhi reached down and put the toy and harness on the nightstand and rolled into my arms. We gently rubbed our juices into each other's skin, teasing each other with wet fingers while licking and sucking playfully, reveling in our moment together. I started tearing up; my emotions welling.

Rhi felt me shake and pulled me into her arms gently. She lifted my chin up and kissed me hard. I let her control the moment, enjoying the feeling of her lips pressed against mine.

"I love you, too, honey." That was all that was needed.

We fell asleep wrapped skin on skin. I knew I didn't want to be anywhere in the world at that moment but in her arms.

Chapter 9

~Little Gidding~

The dove descending breaks the air
With flame of incandescent terror
Of which the tongues declare
The one discharge from sin and error.
The only hope, or else despair
Lies in the choice of pyre of pyre-
To be redeemed from fire by fire.
Who then devised the torment? Love.
Love is the unfamiliar Name
Behind the hands that wove
The intolerable shirt of flame
Which human power cannot remove.
We only live, only suspire
Consumed by either fire or fire.

Excerpt from Four Quartets by T.S. Eliot

Rhianna~ I awoke to the sound of drumming, a faint rhythmic pulsing. Fingers tapping, slamming against animal skin stretched taught over a round frame. I'd know the sound anywhere. Handmade Indian drums. Someone was calling my cell phone and the music that was playing was a song I had assigned to my Uncle Tom (Two Feathers). "The Ghost Song" by The Doors." I reached over and grabbed the phone and looked down at the caller ID then hit answer. The music kept right on playing.

Hello? Hello? I repeated three or four times, but there was only static then silence. I hit the end button and waited, rubbing the sleep from my eyes. It wasn't unusual for the connection to suck from the reservation. It had happened before. I figured he would try again or I would dial him back.

The phone rang again and I hit the answer button:

"Hello.. Hello..? I repeated.

This time I heard something far different, the sound of whistling coming through the speakers. It was hesitant at first then more pronounced, there was no mistaking the song, but this time it was with voice...

Ring-a-ring o' roses,
A pocketful of posies,
A-tishoo! A-tishoo!
We all fall down
Cows in the meadows
Eating buttercups
A-tishoo! A-tishoo!
We all jump up.

A child's voice, a woman's voice, and a man's voice they all filtered in and out over the speaker filling the room with the song before the connection dropped and went dead again.

I looked at the phone now freaking out and hit the redial button trying to call Uncle Tom back, but the phone just rang and rang. I hung up and touched the phone looking at the call log. No one had called? Okay, that was fucking freaky. Then I heard a noise like something slamming into the house. I could hear the wind howling outside as the whole building started shaking. I looked around confused and I'm not too proud of a bitch to say I wasn't just a little bit more freaked and frightened at that point.

I rolled over and found Misty sound asleep next to me. I tried to rouse her from her slumber, but she stayed asleep. I pushed her back and spanked her ass, but she didn't move. I reached over to the nightstand and grabbed my gun, just in case. All my senses were dialing up as I stepped onto the floor and carefully padded my way across to the bedroom door grabbing the handle I pulled it open ready to fire. The coast was clear, I blew a strand of blonde hair out of my face and walked carefully into the living room.

The soft glow of a lamp greeted me. I could hear the wind moving the trees outside. I stepped across the floor checking and rechecking, listening for anything out of the ordinary. That's when I heard the sound of an owl hooting, calling from the back porch. I went to the curtains and peered out and saw Mephisto sitting on his perch.

"What are you doing here?" I said.

109

I didn't have him this week. The owl spun his head to look at me while bouncing on his perch. My alarms started going off because he shouldn't be here. He screeched and flew toward the window with his claws out.

I leapt back as the bird impacted the window and his claws came through the glass like nails causing small cracks everywhere. Mephisto was shrieking as I looked around. Something wasn't right.

Suddenly, the floor beneath me went black and the light in the living room started to flicker and buzz. It was a chilling effect, like an old Frankenstein movie when the doctor turned on the generators to reanimate the corpse. Fuck at this point I wouldn't be surprised at anything!

"Think Rhi! What's going on?" I muttered.

Then it dawned on me. I was in dream world again. I was dream walking.

Suddenly, it was like I fell through a doorway and dropped. I let out a scream still holding my gun tightly as I hit metal and slid down a chute. I slid really fast and suddenly I was ejected into the air and landed in a pile of what I thought was sand. I kept my gun out and rolled out quickly from the pile looking around for targets. The area was black again. Then one by one torches flared lighting a tunnel in front of me. It looked like I was being summoned. Fuck this was some creepy shit.

I could use some backup.

I looked around, but I couldn't see anything above or behind me. It was just a black void. I looked down at the pile, and my skin started to crawl. I could see bones peaking out and what looked like a skull. My hand trembled as I reached down and pulled the skull out. A gold tooth shined in the torchlight. I dropped it back into the pile looking at my hand. It wasn't sand, it was ashes. My stomach turned at the thought of landing in cremated bodies. I bent over retching then straightened up and looked down the tunnel.

I walked forward down the lit corridor. It looked vaguely familiar. There were markings on the wall. I stopped to read at the inscriptions; it looked like cuneiform or Indian cave drawings or something similar. I could make out what looked like a monster breathing fire and hunters throwing spears or shooting arrows. The images were very worn with age. I ran my fingers over the stone walls, but kept walking down the tunnel holding my gun at the ready.

I could see the bullets peeking out from the cylinder; I'd made sure the gun was fully loaded. I stopped to check and see what else I was carrying. I found my knife in my boot and I was fully dressed. Now, I was sure I was dream walking! I had been nude when we had gone to sleep.

I carefully peeked out the end of the tunnel. I saw a chain link fence and gate in front of me. There were two metal signs mounted to the chain links, one said "Keep Out" the other said "We All Fall Down..."

My heart was racing a mile a minute. I was back in the Diablo Canyon again, but the dream was different. I saw a large bonfire burning in a clearing. It was as if the light of the fire was contained. There was only an inky blackness beyond. I pushed open the gate, the hinges creaked as I walked over to the fire, keeping my gun trained, looking for a target.

Suddenly, the air shimmered by the flames and a figure appeared squatting by the fire. It looked like a man dressed in animal skins and leather buckskin. I circled to the left, keeping my gun trained on him, but he did not look up. I noticed as I circled toward the front, the view never changed, it was like I was stuck in a loop of some kind. The image of the man kept glitching. I finally stopped when I realized there was no advantage to be gained since I could not see his face. I stepped into the light of the fire. The man looked up and that was when I realized it was my Uncle Tom.

"Hello Rhi," he said softly. I was still on my guard as I walked over to the figure.

"Hello, Two Feathers. What brings me to you this evening?"

He looked and sounded just like my uncle. He was even dressed in his customary ritual clothing.

"In my walks I have seen the beautiful Raven stretching her majestic wings and soaring farther afield. The spirits told me you could use my guidance," he continued in his calm voice that always soothed my soul.

112

"I can, Uncle, and what else did they tell you?

My uncle stood to his full height and pulled out a large wooden staff with a glowing light on the end. He pointed at the ground near the edge of the clearing.

"Watch, young one!" he said firmly.

The air started glowing and coalescing before an orange mist formed. I kept my eyes on the spot until finally a human form started to materialize. After a few more minutes, the air stopped and a man stepped out. I couldn't fucking believe it. I looked at my uncle.

"Why the fuck would you bring him here?" I asked, yelling at my uncle.

"Look at him," my uncle said. "See him for what he truly is."

"Hello, Rhi…Rhi…Rhianna," he stuttered.

My uncle looked at me with a blank expression. I couldn't read him like I usually could. This frightened me as my uncle was always good at saying what was on his mind, even if half of his tales were old in riddles.

"Don't fear him," my uncle said. "Study him. See him. Even those who walk in the shadows may eventually find light."

I didn't understand. What the fuck was he talking about? Why had he brought this man to me?

Panic overrode my instincts. I was in the café again with Misty when she had spoken to him only briefly. My skin was crawling as he stepped forward and stuck out his hand.

"P…p…pleased   to   m…meet   you.   I'm K…Kevin," he stated.

I kept back peddling. My uncle watched closely. I reached down and grabbed my knife from my boot and faced Kevin or whatever it was.

"Come closer and I'll cut you ear to ear." I threatened, looking menacingly at Kevin.

"Don-n't you, you know kn-kniv-knives are-e dan dan-ger-ous!" he said, reaching a finger out.

The man held a hand out as if wanting me to shake it. I slashed at the hand and heard a loud expletive as Kevin grabbed his hand. Blood started coming out, and he looked at me with a wounded expression on his face.

"Wa…wa…why did you do that?" he asked.

He looked confused and possibly sad.

"I know you ran into a Skinwalker, Rhi. Remember the stories I told you about them? They are members of my tribe and others that have crossed over, giving blood relatives as payment to live and work their evil. They weave lies to cover their tracks; they kill to keep the horrible secret of what they have become. Their humanity has been stripped from them," he said gravely.

I looked at the blood oozing from Kevin's hand. I tore my shirt and wrapped it around his hand. I kept whispering I'm sorry.

"So they exist in two worlds?" I asked.

"Yes," my uncle answered.

"So, the last one I faced was a Skinwalker? Then what's going on back home?"

"You have someone or something that knows you can see, yet what you have seen is clouded by their magic. Sometimes, the walkers will project themselves onto others to throw off their pursuers," he replied.

"So the murders I saw on television, is that a Walker?" I asked.

My uncle didn't get the chance to answer.

"Wha...wha...why did you c...c...cut me?" Kevin asked.

"Why did you cut me?" came a strange raspy voice, like that of an old lady.

"Why did you do that?" repeated another voice, this one sounding like a man in a great deal of pain.

"Why did you do that?" came a third voice.

"WHY DID YOU FUCKING DO THAT?!" this one sounded like a young boy.

My uncle looked up at the sky and began turning

115

in all directions as if searching for the source of the voices. Kevin didn't budge. He remained there with his hand outstretched, blood seeping from it, and I suddenly felt guilty for cutting him. I reached out to touch his hand and lightning shot from the sky, hitting the ground behind him. Dirt kicked up with a shower of sparks.

In the spot where the lightning had touched down, a wooden cross now stood, and on it was a young boy. His hands were nailed to the planks and his dirty feet dangled down at the bottom, below black slacks. His blue shirt rippled in the wind. He couldn't have been older than eleven or twelve. His hair nearly covered his dark eyes, black pools of evil.

"You must go," my uncle yelled at me. "Go now."

"FUCKING GO!" the young boy yelled and from his mouth blew a gust for rotten wind.

The stench of it caused me to take a step back.

"Leave it alone!" came a voice to my right. "Or I'll rip apart your soul and fuck your rotting corpse."

Her face was no farther than a foot from mine. She had no teeth but soft, decaying gums in their place and she smiled a wicked grin. A crown of razor wire dug into her head.

The sound of teeth chomping at my left ear made me fall back onto my ass. A demon of sorts jumped at me, chomping his jagged, broken teeth an inch from my face.

"Stay away!" he screamed.

I didn't have to look behind me to know another presence was there, waiting for me to turn around. I refused.

"Uncle," I said.

My uncle smiled at me.

"Go!" he yelled, and for the first time, I saw fear on his face. "Your dreams are part of the circle, but the answer is not there. Come to the reservation, Rhianna that is where you will find your answers. Now, run!"

Suddenly, the air started to shimmer and lighten. The circle of light around the fire started to expand.

"Run Rhi! They know you are here! Remember, they can take your life here or in the real world!" he yelled.

"What about you?" I replied, reaching for his hand.

"They will catch you if you pull an old fox along, hurry!" he yelled.

My uncle waved his staff and Kevin faded. I sprinted for the fence, leaping into the air and kicking the gate open, before running down the tunnel. I heard the sound of footsteps again coming behind me. I didn't look back. I leaned forward and ran harder. I saw the pile of ashes I had landed in before looming in front of me. The inky blackness beyond was waiting. The sound of pursuit, the sound of panting, they were drawing closer and closer. I could see the shadows from the flame light the walls.

I didn't know what was ahead but I jumped onto the pile and threw myself forward as I felt something grabbing me again. It was like before; I free fell in the blackness and saw my body lying in the bed rushing up to greet me. It wasn't a merging, more like slamming into a door or wall as my eyes fluttered open and waves of pain flooded across me. I was back in my bed. I looked up at the skylight and could see the faint tendrils of sunlight teasing the edges of the glass. I reached over and felt Misty next to me. I wrapped myself around her body and inhaled her scent. It was sweet and full of sex. I felt her push back against me. It felt so good to hold her. She was my safe place. I was going to have to process this dream for a minute. There was so much to take in. I was afraid to look at my back again.

If Misty saw it she would freak. Luckily Royston was in the spare room, when we got up I would tell them both what had happened. For now, I needed to catch my breath and process it all like my uncle had taught me. I held onto Misty tightly until my breathing had returned to normal. I watched the sun slowly rise. She would be up soon. She always was.

Chapter 10

~The Dry Savages~

There is no end, but addition: the trailing
Consequence of further days and hours,
While emotion takes to itself the emotionless
Years of living among the breakage
Of what was believed in as the most reliable-
And therefore the fittest for renunciation.
There is the final addition, the failing
Pride or resentment at failing powers,
The unattached devotion which might
pass for devotion less,

In a drifting boat with a slow leakage,
The silent listening to the undeniable
Clamour of the bell of the last annunciation.

Excerpt from Four Quartets by T.S. Elliot

Royston~ The alarm went off on the phone. The sound of Big Ben rang throughout the room. I reached over and tapped the snooze button, wanting more rest, but as is always the case, my mind was like a blender being turned on for the morning smoothie. Once the clock chimed, it was off to the races I'm afraid. I rolled onto my back and stared up into the skylight, mulling over the last few days. I still didn't have an answer as to who paid the boys for the prank, but I didn't want to upset Rhi and Misty anymore.

The back-to-back shows were a welcome distraction and having our friends here had really helped buoy Rhianna's spirit. I would have to talk with Abel and Elias and see if they would want to release any of the tapes. I had saved a rough mix off of the sound board and also used a HD recorder to record a live mix from the show at Red's. Maybe we could do a Jimmy Page with the Black Crowes kind of thing.

I knew our fans; there would be bootlegs of the show out. Better to get higher quality recordings out rather than those. I hadn't heard from Reid or Mac lately? I hadn't really even had time to watch the news to see if there were any further developments on the Simple Simon case. I rolled out of bed and checked my phone. It was a bloody business and the blighter always used the pie ingredients in the bodies.

There were some similarities to the case in England. Maybe it was a copycat crime, but some of the specifics of the murders were too similar. The police at the time had omitted certain facts that had been given to the press, yet in reviewing the autopsy reports that Mac had given me, I had found correlations with my father's old case. They weren't perfect though, leading me to believe it was a copycat or someone that was familiar with the details.

I rubbed my chin and eyes. Of course it could just be a coincidence; it wouldn't be the first time that had happened. Most serial killers were smart men and women. They had to be to cover their tracks so effectively. My father has always said;

"Don't make the facts fit the theory; you go where the facts take you. If they deviate then they deviate. A good detective gathers all and sorts through the business as he is gathering clues. No matter what the similarities, never assume two cases are related until proven otherwise by the facts of the case. More than one case had gone to ribbons based on suppositions and police incompetence."

The McMartin Preschool case in California came to mind immediately.

We had the winery show tonight. I would have to ask Rhianna which songs she wanted to do for the set. The crowd was going to be upscale and highbrow, not that we hadn't played at private parties, but I knew Derek was probably going to have some specific selections for the good doctor. I pulled up the text message and reviewed the Damian Cellars Winery and everything I could find out about our host on my phone.

Private vineyard, there was some information

discussed on the play boards online but not much. When Derek had said invite only, I think silence was part of the invite. At the very least, a need for discretion from the guests not to share Forests business or sexual predilections or the goings on at the residence were all requirements. The man knew how to cover his tracks. I wondered what bit of snooping he would have me do regarding the sex traffickers. They were a nasty lot, quick to pull the trigger and leave bodies lying about so that others would know not to meddle in their affairs.

They were not averse to murdering the civil authorities if they got to close to their business. I was going to have to tread lightly when it came to this bit of hacking. I threw on a set of bicycle shorts and a AC/DC t-shirt and headed down the stairs to the kitchen. I was sure a whistling teapot would rouse Rhianna and we could go over some of the show details while I made breakfast. Hopefully, her pantry was stocked and I could whip up a quiche or something favorable for everyone.

Being a good cook never hurt and I was one of the few men that Rhianna allowed kitchen privileges too. I wanted to go by Ava's place to check in with her and Laura. Maybe I would text Mac and Reid later, but our schedule today was full even if Napa was only an hour away, and we would need time to get prepared. Derek had messaged me that Forest had made all the arrangements for the sound and lighting for us and the other bands and taken our suggestions at face value and everything was done. I called our costume shop and made arrangements for Tilly to have some special accessories ready for Rhianna's show tonight. I would stop by in the bus to pick them up round back. It was our standard arrangement.

I filled the red teapot and flipped on the burner on the Wolfe stove. I washed the few dishes that were in the sink and checked my email while waiting for the water to boil. The pot started to whistle, and I let it run for about 30 seconds before removing the pot. That should be enough to wake the house. I pulled down some cups and saucers and poured my cup and set a tea thimble filled with earl grey into the boiling water watching the water cloud as the tea was absorbed, releasing the tasty ingredients. I heard a door open and footsteps from the bedroom area. I looked at my watch as Rhianna came padding into the kitchen wearing pajama bottoms and a loose fitting Nirvana T-Shirt. I gave her a smile.

"Good morning my dear. I thought the whistling pot would rouse you from your slumbers," I said then carefully handed her the cup of tea.

"Morning Royston." She mumbled back taking the cup. She set it on the counter and gave me a tight hug. "I had another dream last night," she told me.

My ears perked up at the word dream and the sleepy look on her face.

"Did you sleep at all? Was it a nightmare?" I asked back casually.

"It was another freaky dream, but my uncle was in it and so was that whistler asshole as well," she said gruffly.

"Let's go to the dining room and have a chat then," I told her.

Rhianna nodded and we walked into the dining room and I sat down with her. She stretched and then rubbed her eyes. I knew from past experience to be patient. The words would come when she was ready. I just sipped my tea and waited.

"So you remember that first dream I had..." was how she started. I nodded my head leaning forward as she recalled the first dream and reminded me about her back. Then she told me about last night's dream recalling everything in vivid detail. There were similarities, but this time there were others involved. One point did stand out though.

"Did you say you got pushed?" I asked.

Rhianna nodded.

"It felt like it," she replied.

"Let me see your back and shoulders, keep your front covered," I replied.

She stood and turned her back to me. I carefully lifted her shirt and looked at the soft skin. There on the top right was a handprint or something along with scratch marks.

"Don't move!" I commanded her. I pulled out my phone and took pictures.

"What did you find?" she asked.

"Be honest, was this from last night with you and Misty?" I asked.

Rhianna started laughing. "No we didn't scratch each other although I bit her ass Royston," she said giggling.

I gave her a smile and showed her the pictures. She kind of shivered. I watched as the skin cleared just like before. I took more pictures recording the process until the marks were gone.

"You said your uncle said to come see him right?" I asked her.

"Yes, just before they came for me. That was the first time we had ever dreamed together. Let me get my phone and see if he did call last night," she told me. She ran into the master bedroom and returned shortly.

"Ok this is weird. There were two calls from him last night," she said. "I remembered answering the phone like I told you."

I asked to see her phone and saw two messages as well. I looked at the time stamp right after each call. Rhianna saw the messages and grabbed her arms.

"I told you what happened. I don't know what to think," she said.

I hit the play icon and listened to the first message. It was silence and static like in her dream.

I went down to the second message and hit the play button. This time I could hear music. There was no mistaking the tune. It sounded just like what was on the tape recorder. We listened a few more times and then stopped.

"The call came from your uncle's phone though?" I asked.

"That's what it looks like Royston," Rhi replied looking perturbed.

I rubbed my chin. I forwarded the message to my phone and took pictures of the time stamp when the call came in and any other information I could find regarding the call.

"Your grandmother has friends on the reservation. Has she heard anything regarding your uncle?" Royston asked.

"No he has been reported missing by the tribal council. The police are looking for him."

"While the authorities are looking for him, we have a show tomorrow, and then our schedule is open. Why don't we go to the reservation with Misty and maybe Detective Logan if the tribal police don't turn up anything?" I asked quietly.

"Sounds like a plan," Rhianna quick replied.

Misty came out of the bedroom and joined us. I got up and started the Keurig coffee machine. I knew she wouldn't be drinking tea. According to Misty tea was for lightweight's that couldn't handle their caffeine. After a few minutes, the ready light came on. I stepped out of the kitchen and smiled at her.

"Machine is ready for whatever your pleasure is this morning," I said to her cheerily.

Misty gave me the eye and grinned.

"What, I don't get coffee served to me Royston?" she asked and put her hands on her hips. Laughter filled the room.

"How about some Kona black?"

I smiled and went back in and made her a cup. I couldn't stand the stuff, it was foul. There was nothing like a good hot cup of tea, but I couldn't make Misty see that.

I set the steaming hot cup down on a coaster in front of her and rejoined them at the table.

"I was planning on making a quiche for breakfast for everyone that is if you're agreeable, then we can meet up with Abel and his family and drive down to Napa. The show starts mid-afternoon into early evening and we could get setup.

"Sounds like a plan Royston. Just do me a favor, I want lots of hot sauce on my quiche," she told me.

I wrinkled my nose at her.

"Must you wreck a perfectly good quiche by dousing it in Tabasco sauce?" I inquired.

"Fuck yes. That's the only way to eat any kind of egg," she replied.

I just shook my head. We heard the guest bedroom door creak open, and Elias and Genevieve came out.

"Did we wake you?" I inquired.

"Naw, we both wanted coffee and heard Rhi's teapot whistling. We figured everyone was up," Elias said.

I clapped my hands together.

"Well then, I shall whip up some breakfast and you can all relax," Royston told them.

I went into the kitchen and set to work. Misty joined me after a few minutes and started cutting up fruit.

"You don't want to relax?" I asked.

"Royston you know me. Besides Rhi and Elias are sitting at the piano playing "The Lovers." Rhi wants Elias to duet with her on the song when we play it at today's gig. He's never heard the song before," she explained.

"Well thank you my dear, this will go quickly then." We busily set to work and before long the quiche was baking in the oven and the fruit tray was chilling in the refrigerator.

I made Potatoes O'Brien as a side along with

croissants to round out the meal. I grabbed a bottle of Tabasco sauce out of the door and set the dining room with Misty. I could hear Elias and Rhi trading vocal lines. They actually sounded quite good. I don't think the song had ever been done as a duet. Hopefully the fans would appreciate the newer version.

The oven timer went off and I retrieved the quiche from the oven. It was perfect. I set it on a rack and allowed it to cool before taking it out into the dining room.

"Hey, breakfast!" Misty announced to them.

I just shook my head. I was going to have to go over the finer parts of dining with her at some point. One doesn't sound like a New York cab driver during certain functions. Misty could care less.

We sat down to eat and the conversation turned light and comforting. About midway through the meal, Elias's phone chimed. He looked down and read the message.

"I was wondering now that all of you have gotten your beauty sleep, if you wanted to stop by my place so we can caravan down to Napa. I was thinking we could check out the place and fuck around before the show?" He read to us.

We all laughed. Elias typed in a quick response that he relayed to everyone.

"Told him we will be there in thirty, Asshat!"

Elias's phone chimed again. He read the response

aloud while everyone chuckled.

"Fucktard!" was the one word response.

Chapter 11

~*East Coker*~

O dark dark dark. They all go into the dark,
The vacant interstellar spaces, the vacant into the
vacant,
The captains, merchant bankers, eminent men of
letters,
The generous patrons of art, the statesmen and the
rulers,
Distinguished civil servants, chairmen of many
committees,
Industrial lords and petty contractors, all go into the
dark,
And dark the Sun and Moon, and the Almanach de
Gotha
And the Stock Exchange Gazette, the Directory of
Directors,

And cold the sense and lost the motive of action.
And we all go with them, into the silent funeral,
Nobody's funeral, for there is no one to bury.
I said to my soul, be still, and let the dark come upon
you
Which shall be the darkness of God. As, in a theatre,
The lights are extinguished, for the scene to be
changed
With a hollow rumble of wings, with a movement of
darkness on darkness,
And we know that the hills and the trees, the distant
panorama
And the bold imposing facade are all being rolled
away-

Excerpt from Four Quartets by T.S. Elliot

Genevieve~ The drive to Napa was beautiful. It had been ages since we had been to the wineries. We had gone with Elias's parents back when we were in college. It was a pleasant memory of a bygone era.

This event was a little more upscale, luckily I had packed accordingly when we had left and had a beautiful white cocktail dress to wear for Elias. I know my man had packed a gun metal gray suit with black button up shirt and matching tie for the after party. The look was going to be hot.

I think the boys had decided to go classic rock for the stage look with blue jeans, boots, v neck tee's and sun glasses. It was always fun listening to them go at it. It was like they had both found their youth again and there was a look in their eyes and a smile that I hadn't seen in years. Elias glanced over at me and smiled as we drove, his hand naturally slipping to my leg and squeezing, stroking the soft skin. He knew it drove me crazy ever since we reunited the day I had landed in LAX. My body responded to his touch immediately. He just had to look at me with his smoldering eyes, and I was soaked in seconds. He had such an effect on me.

We were all carpooling out of Sausalito. Royston had texted the address to Forest's place, so Abel was leading the charge up the 101 North. Gia sent us a group text message that traffic was awful and we would be detouring around. Patience was not one of Abel's strong suits, but with his whole family in tow, I couldn't blame him. An hour drive taking two, three or more hours can wear on you if the baby starts fussing. I couldn't get over that Abel was a father. The role suited him well. He had truly become a protector and guardian and he took the role very seriously.

Elias had messaged Khyentse before we had left so our security detail would be stashed somewhere around keeping an eye on things. We hadn't told Abel the extent of the shit that had gone down yet and he knew Elias had security lurking, but we kind of left it unsaid as to where they were. It was better that way. I'm sure the two of them were going to have a heart to heart at some point, but even after living through what had happened, I sometimes had trouble wrapping my brain around what Elias had become. It was like right out of a comic book.

Khyentse had gone to a lot of trouble to make it look like Elias was still at the Mesa compound or traveling to Los Angeles. He had even hired a double to fill in so the cameras would see what looked like my honey going to work, getting out of limousines and doing the day to day shit. It was all carefully orchestrated, but after our vacation we were going to have to deal with Qaylin and his mother again. Better for them to think things were normal and we had just beefed up security, then to come here and make another attempt at taking me. I was grateful for the illusion of normalcy that we were having together.

Elias popped a CD into the rental cars changer and before long the opening track from Shadow and Flame's debut album came on. The album was really beautifully crafted. Rhianna was an exceptional songwriter, but her band is what really made the whole album shine. The opening track "Tear Down The Walls" was heartfelt, but left you wanting more. You could tell it was written by someone who had a lot of bad relationships. I know the fans thought it might be a reference to governments sealing borders with their neighbors, but Rhianna never struck me as someone that would be that political.

I knew a bit about Misty and Rhianna's past and how they had finally settled and really fell in love with each other. The second track "The Rising" was a chugging thundering exclamation point of music that powered the heart and soul. It was about not letting someone keep you down. It almost had a Springsteen kind of feel to it.

Elias drummed the steering wheel while his fingers slid up my dress and found my inner thigh. I could tell he was going to keep me dialed up fully before the show. I let out a small moan and pushed forward with my hips. He reached up and cupped me through my thong as the keyboard and guitar started for the band's song "The Lovers." It really was beautiful as he teased my wetness, but wouldn't slide my panties aside and give me relief. He loved being in control of my body, and I loved giving it to him.

The words were like springtime, like new love in bloom. I know it sounds poetic, but Rhianna really poured her heart into the track. I'm sure Misty had something to do with it. The track wove in and out from soft to soaring with the vocals and instruments building to a nice crescendo then falling back into the melody and verse. It was a brilliant bit of songwriting the lyrical quality reminded me of ABBA back in their hay day.

Elias's fingers pressed down on my pussy, teasing me even more. I moaned loudly and then he cupped me again glancing down at me and smiled.

"Don't worry G, I will take good care of you later, I promise," he said.

"Baby," I said. My pussy was aching for more of his attention. I slid down in the car seat. He smacked my thigh and told me to sit up.

"We are in wine country already and I don't want you to miss out. It's changed quite a bit since we were here," he said smiling.

I begrudgingly obeyed. I knew he would paddle my ass if I got to out of hand. Come to think of it, a good paddling would feel good right about now. I let my mind play with the thought as I pulled my dress down and peered out the windows. He was right, it was beautiful. Wineries lined both sides of the highway with the grape vines climbing the beautifully terraced hills. Some of the vineyards were in the flat of the valley with others on the terraced hillsides. It was still winter, so the vines had not leafed out or blossomed yet. I always liked seeing the vines in bloom. Elias hit the turn signal and we exited the two-lane highway then turned onto a side road following Abel's lead. Rhianna and Misty were in the SUV behind us, and Royston was bringing up the rear in the tour bus with Jez and Ace.

We drove up the road and saw a set of large steel gates. It almost looked Victorian or English.

"What is this place? I don't recall ever seeing this winery when we toured Napa last time?" I asked.

"It's called Damien's Cellars. It's a private winery," he replied.

"Oh? So they don't sell to the masses?" I said demurely.

"I don't know that much about Forest. Remember we are coming as guests with Rhianna. I'm sure Royston knows the lowdown on this guy. I could have Khyentse run a full background check on him through the public channels, but Royston will know what's not available if you're curious, I'm sure they will be serving wine for you to sample baby," he replied with a smile on his face.

I playfully pinched his side.

"Smart ass, I was just curious," I replied.

The road changed from asphalt to gravel to pea gravel. We crested a rise and we both gasped at the beauty of the vineyard. Mustard was in bloom, the bushy plant filling the space between the rows of vines to keep the weeds out. At the head of each row, beautiful rose bushes displayed their blooms. It was absolutely stunning the colors that were on display. Between the yellow of the mustard and the red and white of the roses, it really was an eloquent display of landscaping. I was going to have to ask Forrest who did the work for him. Maybe they could come down to Mesa and do something similar at Elias estate.

With the tires crunching over the crushed gravel, we continued around the perimeter of the palatial estate and stopped in a parking lot out back filled with luxury cars. Forest had sent Royston directions, I'm sure he had sent them to Abel. The lot was filled with Bentleys, Porsche's, an Aston Martin, a Porsche Pan America, a Ford GT 250 was boxed in by two Lamborghinis and a Ferrari. Add in Mercedes Benz, Maseratis, and the ever present Jaguars and of course a Vintage Bugatti from the 40's all in black with walnut trim. There was a lot of space between each car to prevent damage I'm sure. Every car sparkled like a diamond, the detailing was flawless. One of the attendants directed Royston and the tour bus off to a separate area. Golf carts with trailers were already waiting to move equipment. I let out a low whistle and grabbed Elias hand before we got out.

"This guy doesn't miss a beat honey," I said.

We joined up with Rhianna and Misty and walked over to Abel's SUV. He hopped out looking at the place.

"Dude, this guy's got serious coin. This place is like wow and he might have a play area downstairs? I can hardly wait to peel my eyes back and see what his idea of a good time is," he said raising an eyebrow and looking at both of us smirking.

Gia came around with Chance and the baby as Misty and Rhianna walked up.

"So what do you think?" Rhianna asked.

"I think this is going to be one of the nicest gigs you are ever going to play, Rhi," Elias said.

Abel rubbed his fingers together.

"Normally these gigs are serious coin. We're talking more than you would make on the door at any given show," he told Rhi.

Rhi smiled at Abel as Misty slid her arm around her girl.

"Let's go find where we are supposed to be, but judging by those tents over there that would be a good place to start."

An attendant led us over to the carts and we all hopped in. Royston was already handling the movement of our gear to the stage.

"I'll meet you there!" Royston yelled to us.

Rhianna and Misty gave him the thumbs up and we were soon making our way to the tents. We arrived just in time to hear the band Angel Fire take the stage. The sound was spot on as we exited the carts they tore into their set.

We all gathered together before heading into the tents. Abel leaned over and whispered to us.

"This dude has some clout, Elias. Angel Fire is a large venue band now. They don't do small gigs. They've been on top of the charts over the last few years and they're one of the hottest rock bands working the circuit. I'm talking thirty, forty to fifty thousand seat venues and huge festivals," he said to us.

"I'm no slouch, I still sell out everywhere I play, but you have to be cha-ching popular with everyone to pull out that kind of crowd," he rumbled.

We walked into the tent and to something unexpected. The stage wasn't some little affair; we're talking full size arena stage with ramps, amps, effects, and lights. The tents formed a semicircle with the stage in front and chairs neatly lined radiating outwards. There was an open dance floor right in front. Kids held up cell phones recording as the band tore into their main hit Hearts Insanity.

It had been all over the radio and MTV and VH1. I mean the band was world-wide famous, not local. Blaze and Spike were tearing up the guitars, their keyboardist was laying down a haunting melody, and the drummer was a whirlwind of pounding motion. The crowd though small was making it up in enthusiasm. The teenagers were losing their minds taking pictures and recording and singing along. We watched from the back partaking on some of the food, a waiter came by offering chilled wine. Another came by with cold beers. We grabbed refreshments as Royston right on cue joined us. He pointed to a blocked off area of the stage with a tent entrance.

"Whenever everyone is ready we can go through there. The sound crew is top notch; they got us setup in record time. When it's time to hit the stage, we'll be ready. I already moved your guitars to the racks. Ace and Jez are making final adjustments. We literally will just roll our gear out, plug in and go," he said.

We all nodded as a big lumbering tower of a man came walking over to us. The man towered over all the men; he could have been a Viking. He extended his hand and introduced himself.

"Thank you for coming down, I'm Forest Summers. You must be Rhianna and Misty," he stated and shook their hands.

I looked at Royston who smiled.

"I gave Mr. Summers our guest list everyone," he exclaimed.

Forest walked over to Abel and Elias and grabbed their hands. The man was massive with huge hands that almost looked like bear paws.

"It's an honor to have you both here. Abel, I've been a fan of your music for years, both with Metal Insanity and with Lethal Abel." He said shaking Abel's hand. He introduced himself to Gia and Mia and Chance. He had an easy way about him. He was hard not to like. He turned to us.

"Elias, I am very familiar with your work with Metal Insanity and I knew your father Jared as one of my competitors. I'm sorry for your family's loss at his passing. He was always a shrewd businessman. I truly hated having him across the table to negotiate against.

141

Don't get me wrong, it was a friendly rivalry, but you would swear you were haggling with the tax collectors in Jerusalem back in the day. He knew how to swing a deal and make a profit," he said smiling.

Elias and Forest shook hands and then turning to me he gently lifted my proffered hand up to his lips and kissed it gently before greeting me in French. The man was very smooth and he did his homework. I'll give him that. Elias's hand never left my back.

"I'm very familiar with your body of work Madame," he said kindly.

"I've been in attendance at more than one of your fashion shows when you have walked down the runway." His eyes never left mine.

"Why thank you. That is most kind and it's always a pleasure to meet a fan," I replied, returning the gaze. He turned back to Abel and Elias.

"I hope with both of you here that maybe you will grace us with a few tunes from when you two played together? I really want to thank you all for coming down to support the cause against human trafficking. In this day and age, it is something that should be long gone by now. *It* is an issue that is near and dear to my heart," he told us.

We all agreed and finished our introductions and then Forest spotted some more of his friends coming into the tent. Mr. Summers graciously excused himself and continued playing host.

Royston nodded, and a man standing next to Forest started in our direction. He had an important vibe to him, but unlike Forest, yet I couldn't put my finger on why. As the gentleman got close, Royston gestured to Rhianna and Misty.

"Derek is headed this way."

The girls straightened as *Derek* joined our circle.

"Thank you for coming today, and please make yourselves comfortable. As you can see Royston, Forest took all of your suggestions to heart and the sound and lighting system is top notch. I have to tell you there are a lot of excited fans here to see you. Sally has no idea what is coming. She's beside herself right now," he said.

"We are happy to oblige, Derek. Not to cut this short but we need to head backstage to get ready for our set. Thank you again for asking us to play. It is indeed a worthy event for charity and coming to play is the least we can do to help you raise funds," Royston replied smoothly.

Derek nodded and headed back to where Forest stood and as we made our way to the side of the stage past dark suited security guards and walked along the side of the stage as Hearts Insanity was rolling into their finale.

"We're up after Beneath The Burn," Royston yelled.

We waited, watching the number one band in the country if not the world tear through their encore with practiced ease. The kids were jumping up and down like they were on pogo sticks. The girls were screaming at the top of their lungs. Rhianna and Misty crossed their arms. Abel leaned over and spoke to everyone.

"Ain't no big thing, stick to your game. They ain't better then you are Rhi, and with us here you're going to kick the guys in the balls and the women are going to go just as ape shit nuts. This is what's coming for you," he said smiling.

Abel and Elias fist bumped. Roadies were running around as Blaze lifted his guitar up in the air then dropped it. The band joined arms on stage and took a bow as camera phones flashed and some of the ladies tossed flowers onto the stage. A man wearing a headset came over to us.

"Beneath The Burn is next, then you are up. It'll only take a second to check the connections. Royston told us what you normally like to be dialed in at on the board. We can adjust accordingly once you're onstage," he said.

We all nodded as Angel Fire came off the stage. It was like watching ants scurry as the stage was cleared of Angel Fire's gear and Beneath The Burn was signaled to take the stage.

With a roar the crowd went nuts as they plugged in and tore into their set with a vengeance. It was like being in the backwash of a jet engine as the band blended craft with haunting lyrics. The music was tight and new. I had heard their tracks on the radio. Seeing them live was a whole different matter. We waited patiently as they deftly wove through their set and finally encored. The guy with the headset was back and signaled to us letting us know it was time.

With a roar the members of Beneath The Burn exited the stage and the roadies scurried out moving gear and cleaning up. It was amazing to watch. We got the signal and Jez and Ace stood up then nodded. The crowd was chanting, wanting more; jumping up and down. You would swear it was a little mini earthquake as they banged the stage.

Royston watched intently as Jez and Ace went out first with their fists raised. I could see the crowd pointing and the younger fans pushed against the front of the stage. Elias and Abel went out next. Suddenly, people recognized Abel and started taking pictures. Both men plugged in and signaled the soundman they were ready even as they checked their boards and made sure everything was working. Misty kissed Rhianna and then went out with her blue hair flowing behind her and her red guitar around her shoulders reflecting the lighting. The crowd started chanting the band's name as Rhianna came out onto the stage.

Even for a dignified group, everyone was whistling and clapping as Rhianna leaned back and straddled the microphone stand. Her hand went up and then dropped and Elias and Abel both stepped forward and started into one of Shadow and Flames most famous songs "The Lovers." Listening to it in the car and seeing it live was a whole different world.

The boys traded off lead and rhythm while Misty kept a constant pace on the song keeping the rhythm flowing as the boys worked over and under and around fleshing out the song. You would swear they were an orchestra it was just luscious. The women in the crowd were eating it up as Rhianna straightened leaning the stand forward her vocals low almost a growl then sliding into the verses one by one. It was almost poetry or prose, but way different.

She had a command on the audience with the song. It was mesmerizing, painful, beautiful and aching all at the same time. I could see why the band had started picking up radio play with the track. It was that good. The more they got out there, the farther it was going to go. The women that were fans of the band were grabbing the edge of the stage taking pictures and some looked like they were in tears. She pulled back the stand pulling the microphone free, prowling the edges and working the crowd.

Rhianna poured her soul into the song and the fans felt and knew it singing along with her, holding their phones in the air. A few of the men pulled out lighters going full old school. We all watched from the sides taking it all in. I held hands with Gia and Chance singing along with everyone else.

It was a moment I don't think I'll ever forget. Rhianna was on the floor of the stage on her back singing the final pieces her hips arched then falling, hand up pleading. It was intense. When she was done she rolled over and got on her knees. We all waited as she slowly stood up with her fist pumped as the band tore into "Stop The Insanity." The boys were right in their element tearing into the track with Misty. Jez was slamming the bass like she was going to kick the door in, and Ace was pounding the skins hard. It was fucking awesome. Before we knew it the set was up and they linked up and bowed then headed off the stage waving to the fans.

Abel was yelling like a madman.

"I told you to own that shit Rhi and you did! Fuck they want us to come out for more. That is how you fucking do it and you kicked them right in the teeth," he bellowed.

It was a great set. I spoke with Elias earlier and they all decided to let Rhi and the band have the spotlight and just be a part of it, not stealing the thunder from Shadow and Flame. There wasn't enough room in the set list to go full bore, and besides, if Derek and Forest wanted they could come to the big show at the Fillmore and bring their girls with them.

After the show we mingled with the guests and enjoyed the opulent food and wine. Forest invited us to partake of his private cellar later, but both Abel and Elias passed and took a rain check. Rhi and Misty were talking animatedly with the band members from Hearts Insanity and Beneath The Burn. Looks like everyone got along okay. Royston was talking with all of them, handing out cards and shaking hands.

Rhianna and Misty came over to join us.

"Hey Abel you were right. Own the place," she said.

"Yeah?" Abel growled.

"They want us to tour with them as openers," she replied excitedly.

"They asked if Lethal Abel or Metal Insanity might want on the bill," she said smiling.

Abel fist bumped everyone.

"Fuck this might work out. Those guys draw big fucking monster crowds. We could tour and seriously have big balls on the table kind of rock fest," he said.

We wound down with everyone else, and before it got dark we made our escape. Rhianna and Misty were both still reeling with the news. Everyone was in the moment just savoring it. I hoped their managers could work out the details. It could be big for everyone.

We rode back in the golf carts, and Royston had Forest's staff help load up the gear. We jumped into the Vette and waited while we all lined up and formed our caravan again. Before long Royston pulled in behind and with a flash of his headlights we all headed back to Sausalito. Elias loaded the Shadow and Flame CD, specifically the Lovers back on the stereo. Before I could say a word his hand was between my legs. This time I slid my panties down so he could finish what he had started. I don't know who was screaming louder during the song, Rhianna or me.

Chapter 12

~*Burnt Norton*~

The detail of the pattern is movement,
As in the figure of the ten stairs.
Desire itself is movement
Not in itself desirable;
Love is itself unmoving,
Only the cause and end of movement,
Timeless, and undesiring
Except in the aspect of time
Caught in the form of limitation
Between un-being and being.
Sudden in a shaft of sunlight
Even while the dust moves
There rises the hidden laughter
Of children in the foliage

Quick now, here, now, always-
Ridiculous the waste sad time
Stretching before and after.

Excerpt from Four Quartets By T.S. Eliot

Elias~ It was good to relax for a minute. After the back-to-back shows, we had a few days to chill and play tourist before the Fillmore gig. If it was even possible, I felt even closer to my friends but especially with Genevieve. This trip was what we needed, and being with friends again had really opened me back up to how I used to be. There was a freedom in not having any responsibility.

My dad was the one who always carried the mantle of responsibility and I understood now what it was to bear that weight upon my shoulders. I was a *Warrior* now. Having that kind of power at my beck and call was fucking crazy. In the here and now, I just needed to be one of many and not the one. I was just hanging out and not having to make world-changing decisions.

I was grateful to Parker and Khyentse for managing things. Not once did I see our shadow detail. I knew they were in the shadows watching us, but they would only reveal themselves when they were needed and not before. I knew after the trip, G and I had to land and reappear again. Hopefully, the boys figured out what was next and what to do about my brother. I know I wanted to kill him for taking Genevieve, but more important I really wanted to know why. The answers were missing, all I had were questions. Maybe I would get some when I returned. And maybe I could solicit a little help from Royston, he was methodical and a little devious in the information he could obtain off the grid. Royston was away for a day handling the Fillmore gig with Abel's manager. They had already sold out the venue, and after the show at Forest's house, Rhianna's band was on the rise. I didn't know if I could break free from Cain Enterprises to sneak in some shows with Abel, but if Khyentse and Parker could find a way to pull it off, I was all in.

We enjoyed the time off traveling the city, going up to Haight Ashbury and Alcatraz and Fisherman's Wharf. We took the Bart and the cable cars everywhere we could. Mia had a blast. I got to be uncle to her and spoil her just a bit. Abel kept the spoilage to a minimum, but with me and G, he cut us a little slack. We didn't have any kids yet, so Mia was the target.

Gia stayed glued to his hip the whole time. We ate and drank ourselves stupid at times; there was so much to do. We drove down the world's craziest, most crooked street on the planet and went to City Lights bookstore that was made famous by the Beat poets in the 1950's. We even drove down to Monterey Bay and went to the aquarium and Cannery Row, where Steinbeck wrote the novel. We went to Half Moon Bay and just soaked it all in. Fuck, this was probably going to be the last break I had from Cain Enterprises for a while, so we made the most of it. Genevieve was glued to my side just like Gia was to Abel's. I kept her close.

I felt more at peace with myself over the last few days. It was like Tai Chi, I was in the moment flowing from each form. That was my life now, flowing from movement to movement. It was perfect and serene. I had a beauty on my arm in Genevieve, I had happiness in the friends I was surrounded with, and I had serenity. Whether real or imagined, the moment was perfect, and as an added bonus, our love was only growing deeper.

We listened to the local classic rock radio station, and the airwaves were full of news about the Fillmore show; the excitement was building. I would be dishonest if I didn't say I was just as jacked up. I hadn't played in front of a large crowd in years. There was something about the give and take of thousands of voices screaming your name and yelling and singing to your songs that was otherworldly.

Rhianna's house had become like a second home to us. She had told us both that we could come stay anytime we wanted. Her house was our house and vice versa. She handed me a spare key and told me to keep it stashed. She didn't even ask if I needed it; she just said if things went south to come stay at her place. I knew she was intuitive, and after our discussion the other night, I knew she was a dream walker. We sat at the bar, celebrating the night before the Fillmore gig, and I asked about her Uncle Tom and if she had any news.

"No, my grandmother has been quiet. But you remember those dreams?" she said.

"Yes, I remember. Did you have another one?" I inquired.

"Yeah, I think it was my uncle telling me to come find him. It was really a freaky dream. I haven't really talked to Misty about it, but after the Fillmore show, I'm going to grab Misty and Royston and go up to the reservation and see if I can get some answers. He has never been out of touch this long, and I am worried," she said.

I nodded my head in understanding.

"If you need anything, I'm quite well connected." I let the statement hang.

"Yeah, Mr. Elias Cain – President of the Fortune 500," she said laughing back at me.

She saw my face and knew I wasn't kidding.

"Hey, I know you mean that. Seriously, if I need you, I know you have the hook ups. I'll burn up your cell phone in a minute if I need the calvary," she said.

I smiled and tipped my beer to her and we touched the bottles. It was our last night before the show. The TV was playing when Rhianna got a weird look on her face.

"Turn it up! Please!" She yelled. We all stopped drinking and looked at the TV and watched the breaking news story.

"Can you turn the TV up?" Rhianna asked the bartender.

"We begin this evening with breaking news on the urgent manhunt currently underway for serial killer, Simple Simon. Yesterday, authorities confirmed four murders have now been connected with another possible victim just found early this morning. Let's go

to Paul Wesley on the scene where he's waiting with the latest."

"Thanks, Gloria," Paul said. "Paul Wesley and we are live on the scene of what appears to be another gruesome murder of the serial killer Simple Simon." The murder victim was discovered this morning in the alleyway you see behind us, and so far the body has not been moved. The coroner's office has been called in as well as forensic teams from the San Francisco Police Department.

They have been scouring the crime scene gathering evidence according to one detective that we had spoken to but declined to be on camera with us. Your News 9 team has been bringing you live and up to the date coverage as events unfold with this case."

The camera angle widened to show the yellow crime scene tape blocking off a dark alley behind the newscaster. Fire and rescue trucks surrounded the area, flashing red and blue lights on the screen.

"The police on scene have yet to officially answer any questions regarding the victim's cause of death or if Simple Simon has left his calling card. We have received confirmation Simple Simon is indeed placing food items into the wounds of his victims. Police have not released what those food items are as of yet. News 9 will remain on the scene and bring you the latest when it becomes available...Simple Simon met a pie man," Paul paused, a snarky smile crossing his face. "Is this an odd coincidence or a twisted take on a beloved toddler's tale? Back to you, Gloria."

"That's some fucked up shit! Who the fuck does that?" Abel said as the story continued.

"Thank you, Paul. Now, for an update on the Swift Fleet employee who was struck by a car after receiving the call from the killer who dubbed himself Simple Simon. The dispatcher, who told detectives the caller whistled the children's nursery rhyme, Ring around the Rosy, before laughing and confessing to having killed multiple people, has been released from the hospital. She is expected to make a full recovery."

Rhianna went absolutely rigid and so did Misty. Both women covered their mouths.

"The police chief is urging the public to be vigilant about personal safety. A toll-free hotline has been set up if you have any information regarding the investigation please call, 1-888-99-simon. Stay safe Bay Area. And we'll be back after these messages."

I glanced down at my beer but a loud thump caught my attention. I turned to find Abel glaring at Rhianna.

"Didn't you say there was whistling in your weird dreams?" he asked.

Rhianna nodded.

Misty shot into the conversation.

"That weird fucker in the café!" she hissed.

"Could be a coincidence, baby. Let's talk about *it* tonight when we get home," she told her.

158

Misty gave Rhi a weird look.

"What, you know something new?" she asked.

"Not new, just not sure if that's the dude or not now," she hesitated.

Misty took a long pull on her beer and slid her arm around Rhianna. She whispered something too low for me to hear, but whatever it was, Rhi nodded and Misty kissed her cheek. Royston rubbed his chin thoughtfully at the interchange. He picked up his phone and started texting away. The last time we had heard anything about Rhianna and the dreams was a few days ago when she had her interview with the police.

Abel came over to us and leaned in.

"Was that the weird shit you told us about before?" he asked, doing the chin nod at the TV.

"Yeah, although I didn't know it was all that and a bag of fucking monkeys, Abel. I'd been having those weird dreams and told Royston about them. We interviewed with Private Investigator Reid and Detective Logan from the San Francisco Police Department. I told them what I knew. We did run into a weird guy at Ava's café the other day though that whistled that same song," Rhianna explained.

Both of us stared at each other.

"Whoa, what the fuck did you just say?" Abel inquired.

"I said there is a guy that goes to Ava's place that loves to eat pumpkin pie and whistles that song." There was exasperation in Rhianna voice.

Abel stepped back.

"Ok, this just went into the fucking twilight zone," he grunted.

I was feeling the same thing. Granted since my father was murdered I knew what the *fucking twilight zone* felt like. *But why didn't they say anything, if they had actually seen someone that was behaving strangely at the café.*

Royston looked up from his phone.

"I sent a message to Mac and Reid and Detective Logan," he said. "I'm sure there is nothing for us to be alarmed about. It could be a coincidence with that chap in the café."

Abel put his fist in his palm.

"I hope so. I see some weird fuck come near the ladies and I am going to punch and break bones first then ask questions after the fucking facts," he said.

At that everyone smiled. Rhianna thanked everyone for their concern, but like Royston said, it could just be a coincidence.

We finished our beers and caravanned back to Rhianna's place. The news broadcast kind of put a damper on the celebration, but tomorrow was a new day and a big one at that. Royston spent the night at

Rhianna's, using the spare room above the garage, again. I didn't know if he was being protective or lazy, but I had a feeling it was option one on the selection list and I couldn't blame him. The newscast had brought reality back into the fold hard.

Chapter 13

~*Burnt Norton*~

In the knowledge derived from experience.
The knowledge imposes a pattern, and falsifies,
For the pattern is new in every moment
And every moment is a new and shocking
Valuation of all we have been. We are only
undeceived
Of that which, deceiving, could no longer harm.
In the middle, not only in the middle of the way
but all the way, in a dark wood, in a bramble,
On the edge of a grimpen, where is no secure
foothold,
And menaced by monsters, fancy lights,
Risking enchantment. Do not let me hear
Of the wisdom of old men, but rather of their folly,

Their fear of fear and frenzy, their fear of possession,
Of belonging to another, or to others, or to God.
The only wisdom we can hope to acquire
Is the wisdom of humility: humility is endless.

The houses are all gone under the sea,

The dancers are all gone under the hill.

Excerpt from Four Quartets by T.S. Eliot

Rhianna~ If you're an adrenaline junky like me, you live for the moments that get the heart racing and your blood screaming through your veins. This show was the step off the cliff for me, for all of us. It was sliding the goggles on over the eyes and stepping to the edge then swallowing and taking a few deep breaths, looking over the edge and opening your arms to the heavens before jumping off the cliff and free falling into the pit of stardom. Some call it a cesspool, others call it prison, but the ones that have experienced it know it for the good and evil it represents. If you like to perform and for every last one of us that do, it is fucking bliss. It's your dreams becoming reality; it's being able to play and perform and live the life you want. It's about doing what you love and going after it. The Fillmore was the stepping-stone. More famous musicians have played and launched their careers from here than anywhere else in the world.

Royston said that the venue promoters really loved our sound and that if we kept packing the place that we would be headlining at the other Fillmore's across the country. One of the great things about the Fillmore wasn't just the capacity of the crowd, it was also the history. Fuck, I was going to be on a stage that every band and singer I had ever idolized had played on. It was like I was going to rock and roll Mecca. I had seen gigs there, always imagining I would play someday on that stage and now the time had come.

I barely slept last night. Misty literally had to scissor her naked body over mine and hold me down.

I was exhausted from the show at Damian's Vineyard, but this was another level. We were both so tired that Misty had stripped me down and followed suit, joining me in the shower. Afterwards, we just crawled into bed. I knew she was going to ask about the newscast. Before she even started, I volunteered the dream and told her everything. She had just laid her head against my breast and gently stroked my arm as I told her all the details reliving each piece of it. It came out in a rush of emotion, and when it was over, I was oddly at peace. She patted my stomach and looked at me.

"So what does it all mean?" she asked me.

"I think my uncle was sending me a message and telling me to not believe anything that was a coincidence. Make sure I have proof," I replied.

"So how come I freaked out?" Misty asked.

"I had told you about the dream and then you see that buffed out, tattooed guy in the café. Didn't he kind of remind you of the guys we used to date?" I asked.

"Yeah, he did kind of look like Zane my ex now that you mention it. You think between the whistling and maybe PTSD, it was like a trigger?" she asked.

"I'm not sure, but Uncle made sure I understood that the whistler dude was human and had a speech impediment on top of it." I replied.

Neither of us said anything, Misty just gently

suckled and teased my nipple until it was rock hard. I moaned in appreciation even as we rolled into each other's arms and made love gently and tenderly. Hell if I knew what it all meant at that moment,

I just knew I had someone that I loved deeply in my arms and the rest of it, we would figure out. If the whistler was human, a bullet from my father's gun would stop him cold, if he wasn't we were going to need help of another kind. I fell asleep tasting her juices on my lips. I didn't want anything more at the moment then her love and knowing how deeply we cared for each other. I figured we could get through this or anything that was thrown at us.

My uncle had always told me to be a good student and watch and learn. This was one of those times I was watching and learning, but patience was never one of my strong suits.

Royston woke us with the whistling teapot in the morning. The fucker was subtle, but he knew it would pull me out of bed every time. I swatted Misty's ass to wake her and with a loud yelp she rolled over to grab me, but I was already rolling out of bed.

"The red whistle express just sounded. I'm sure Mr. Munt is anxious to get the day started," I said.

Misty gave me a sexy look. I knew it well, it was the common 'honey, let's go one more round and let the boys play' kind of look. I wanted to crawl back into bed, but I knew that everyone would be up early for this gig. This was the whole reason everyone was here and we absolutely had to kill it. No mistakes, no fuckups, we had to be spot on, knock them the fuck into the walls perfect! I reached over and grabbed my girl and pulled her into my arms as my mouth finding hers. I knew that would shut her up on the spot. Our lips parted, tongues danced then we slowly separated her fingers and mine tracing over each other's bodies.

"If this goes off perfect, the black raven is coming out with a vengeance," I said.

Misty bit her tongue and crooked her head and smiled at me.

"Is that a threat or a promise or both?" she asked.

I laughed as we went into the bathroom to get cleaned up prior to throwing on pajama bottoms and t-shirts. We headed out into the living room where Elias and Genevieve were already sitting on the couch drinking coffee.

"Well, look at you two up bright and early," I said.

"Yeah, I was tossing and turning last night. G elbowed me a few times since I elbowed her on accident," he replied.

I gave Genevieve a raised eyebrow and she laughed.

"It's a king size fucking bed for Christ's sake! How much room does the man need?"

We all laughed. Royston came out with a tray of tea.

168

"Coffee is started and should be ready momentarily. I have pastries baking and they should be up as well."

Royston set down the tray and went back into the kitchen. We plopped down next to Elias and G.

"Isn't he Mr. Efficient this morning?" I asked.

"Fuck Rhi, the dude takes good care of you. Why don't you both marry him and just keep him around the place for good?" Elias asked.

At that everyone burst out laughing. Right on queue Royston came walking back into the living room and set down another tray.

"I already messaged Abel and Gia and Jez and Ace. Everyone should be along shortly," he told us quickly.

"Glad I had a say in it," Rhianna replied.

"We have a busy day. I have to meet the lighting crews and stage people at lunch. We need to get setup, and you need to go over the set list for the show. Having everyone here facilitates that. I was grateful that everyone kept their alcohol consumption to a minimum making today that much easier." He sounded a tad more British than usual.

Right on queue the doorbell rang and in came everyone else. Abel was his usual wise ass self.

"So I get a text from Royston to come for breakfast. I asked him if he was Betty Crocker and was the fucker going to be baking, and look what is on the table." He laughed.

Gia followed with Chance, and Mia and Jez and Ace were right behind them. The living room burst into conversation as Royston pulled chairs in from the dining room to accommodate the guests. Everyone helped themselves to the pastries, tea and coffee as we talked about the coming show and how good it had been to see everyone. Sadly, I knew my friends were going to head back down to LA in the morning. That was a real bummer, but I knew from this point forward, things were going to be different between all of us and for the better.

"Hey, I talked to my manager. If Angel Fire was serious about doing some live gigs and Elias is up for it..." Abel interjected glancing at Elias.

"Which part of 'Fuck Yes, I'm In' don't you understand, Abel?" Elias shot back quickly.

We all laughed.

"Does that mean Metal Insanity is going to reform?" I asked them both.

"I don't know about that. I think doing some live shows and getting the brand back in the public spotlight would be a good thing, but I also have to consider my company and how much time I can devote to touring. Abel has been doing this for awhile, so if it's okay with him, slow and easy, but yeah I think it would be good for both of us," Elias said.

"Agreed. Besides, I have to consider the rest of the guys in Lethal Abel. I know they'll love the idea that you and I are playing again, but they're loyal to the brand we have created. So specific shows and shit like that, I think will work," Abel said.

Both guys fist bumped and we all cheered.

Royston came in with a round of shots.

"Whoa, it's too early for that," I said.

Royston laughed and looked at everyone.

"I do believe that we just witnessed Hell thawing after many years. I don't know about all of you, but the thought of these two gents at least touring and playing once in a while after so many years, well... I want a fucking shot! Now who is going to join me?" he asked.

At that, we all clapped hands and grabbed a shot. We tilted them back letting the whiskey burn down our throats, and then we went back to breakfast. The boys talked animatedly. I didn't know if they could pull it off, but at least they were acting like best friends again, even brothers. It was a cool thing to see. I knew Gia and G were happy as well. Losing someone that close in your life just sucks. The fact that shit was patched up, and they were tight again... no words, it was just cool.

Royston handed out a suggested set list. Elias, Abel and I went back and forth with the band deciding on different tracks to play. Metal Insanity had one particular nasty number called "Razor" that would be perfect to start. I had a track called "Rip Out My Heart" that would work next. One by one we picked out the list. Royston had only missed the list by approximately three tracks. Abel had to give Royston props for knowing the material; he had dug up a few jams that hadn't been played in a long time. The fans were going to fucking love the set.

After breakfast we went out to the tour bus and loaded up. Royston had already called ahead, and they had the alley blocked off so we could slip in. Jez and Ace were riding with Royston like before, and the rest of us would caravan in our cars. Abel was going to lead again. He had been to the venue many times over the years with Lethal Abel.

Ace and Jez had packed their stage clothes already in the tour bus. Royston suggested one specific outfit he would like to see me wear for the show, and Misty gave him the thumbs up. Damn it was a short dress. I hoped I didn't sneeze and give the front row a show. I grabbed the metallic blue dress as Misty grabbed her black one. We both laughed. Hopefully with the nylons and panties we wouldn't let too much kitty out of the bag.

"Baby, as long as we're not giving the front row a full show, it's all good," Misty said.

I smiled at my lover as we headed back out to the car with dresses in tow. Royston glanced them over really quick and nodded his approval.

"That ought to incite the crowd, ladies, good

choices." he told them.

We jumped into the cars and headed out. The drive across the Golden Gate was uneventful, but the view was spectacular. There was even a three mast tall ship from the coast guard coming into the harbor. I pointed the ship out to Misty.

"I wonder how many sailors we would have to bone to get a ride on that thing?" she asked in her best slutty voice.

"Misty!" I exclaimed.

My girl laughed as we exited the bridge and followed Abel as we made our way to the corner of Fillmore and Geary Ave. I pulled out my phone and snapped pictures of the marquee as Misty slowed down briefly. We were the headliner, and there in all its glory was "Shadow and Flame Tonight 7:00 PM with surprise special guests." After the events of the last few days, the fans knew who the guests probably were.

The show was completely sold out, and Royston had even arranged to have it taped. Abel was all for it, the Metal Insanity and Lethal Abel fans were going to download and purchase the hell out of it. Royston and Abel's manager had even come up with a shirt design for the show.

We expected to sell out of everything including programs. The local radio stations had signed on to promote the hell out of the show. One of them had a small booth inside for a live broadcast on air, too.

We all parked and hopped out of our cars and made our way inside. The place smelled musty but not gross. The building had been retrofitted and repaired back in the 90's during the earthquake; the owner had wanted the venue to reopen and paid for it out of his money.

The stagehands pointed us to the dressing rooms where we stowed our gear. Royston worked with the crews to get the stage setup. Between the lasers and pyro techniques and high definition LCD screens and stage, the show was going to be ridiculous.

There were no other words. We all went to the main bar area to relax until we were needed. Royston came to grab us after about an hour. The main stage was set up and the light rigging was hung. LCD panels had been fitted across the wooden stage. Ace and Jez started bringing in amps and cabinets. We all pitched in and before long we were ready. Royston made sure we had extra microphone stands and there was a wall of monitor speakers. We had backups to the wireless microphones as well.

The entire stage was computer controlled and was beyond bitchin! I mean it could look like anything we wanted it to. Water, ice, it was like playing on a hologram or something. I kept waiting for Tupac to rise out of the stage at any moment. The crews worked furiously fine-tuning everything. The show was going to be unlike anything anyone had seen since the Dead and The Airplane used to play the joint. Anyone that was tripping balls was going to lose their mind at the show. Security placed a barrier along the front and sides to make sure the crowd didn't break through. In all my years of playing, I had never been on the security side of the fence before; I was always an outsider looking in.

Royston covered the tour bus in the alley and security was posted everywhere. You would think we were rock and roll royalty, but it wasn't long before the manager came to find us.

"They're already lining up in front. You're not even on for another few hours. They're scalping tickets for a few hundred a shot. Standing room only," he informed us.

Royston smiled at the news.

Abel and Elias changed into their show gear. I had to admit it was hot. Black leather pants and boots with open V-neck shirts cut to the middle accentuating their bodies. Big ass skull belt buckles and chains around their neck. The girls were going to rush the stage at the sight of them. I better make sure the dinner crew didn't give Gia a knife. She might wind up cutting a bitch before the night was out.

"You guys look fucking fantastic. I haven't seen those duds since back in the day!" I clapped.

Gia and G both gave the thumbs up sign.

I went with Misty to change and came back out shortly wearing the short blue dress. Misty was in black with a very similar dress. We had slid on sheer nylons and panties to keep ourselves tucked. Even

175

then, I would have to keep the gymnastics to a minimum or show change to jeans and a tee shirt. We had metal overkill going as it was. Elias, Abel and Misty were all on guitars. Jez was on bass with Ace on drums. They had even set up his drum set with some of the lasers so the whole rig glowed when he played it. The stage setup was sick. I mean I had never seen anything like it. I wondered how much we had paid for the setup. Although, Royston wasn't stupid; if he thought this was what was needed, he had my authority to do it. I had to admit what he had brought to the party looked even hotter than the show we had just played in Napa. All I had to do was use my voice to melt the boys and girls alike and we were in like Flynn.

Abel and Elias gave us both the once over.

"What are you Abba?" Abel asked laughing.

"Ha, ha very funny you big ape!" I laughed, flipping him the bird.

Abel and Elias both had to fuck with us. The dresses were short but looked hot. Jez was wearing black and blue pants and a matching top that played off our colors. Ace was wearing a black wife beater and shorts. We settled in and waited as the manager came in with updates.

"Doors opened and we're turning people away. Fake tickets are starting to be tried at the door. Balcony seats are up to $100.00 a seat and that's with obstructed view," he said.

I whistled. The owners had called in backup from SFPD to help. There was a huge crowd outside. So far nobody had done anything stupid, but I knew that Abel could draw them in. I didn't expect this though.

"You ready for this? Once we hit the stage, once we go down this rabbit hole, things are going to start to change Rhi. Just remember we got your back," Abel said, pointing at himself and Elias.

"Thanks guys. You have no idea what this means to me." I started to tear up.

"Off with the water works, we are about to blow the roof off!" Abel exclaimed.

I laughed and gave both guys a hug. The band formed a circle and joined hands. We yelled yes as the house lights dimmed and the crowd started chanting. It was surreal as we peeked out the edges of the curtains. The place was completely jammed full.

The stage manager came over to talk to Royston and pointed at us. A video screen lit up behind the stage and a short promo video that Royston had made of Shadow and Flame appeared. The crowd chanted and hooted, knowing what was coming. We were escorted onto the stage behind the curtain while the video played on the other side. We all plugged in and using our wireless headsets made sure we were on. The video ended and the curtain lifted.

The lights came up on stage, lighting the whole band as we all looked at each other then the fans. I raised my arms as Abel's hands slashed across the strings and started playing one of Metal Insanities more infamous tracks "Razor." Elias was right beside him pulling off leads and hammers as his fingers matched Abel's then soared away.

Misty dropped into the growling main riff of the song, letting the boys cut loose as Jez chopped downward on her bass and Ace slammed into the kit, driving the whole song forward. The stage came alive below and around us. Black ice then flames and all kinds of wicked effects added to the surreal quality as I stepped forward and started singing my heart out to the fans.

~The Razor by Metal Insanity~

Living on the edge of life

Hairs breathe between the razor

The moments that I wanted to give

The ghost that had to live

I fall backwards into the flames

And burn

The razor drew the blood that turns

red dripping from my wrists

I want to scream and …

My voice breaks from the drone screaming as the whole band surges forward. I drop to my knees consumed as we plow into the next chorus and next.

There are no wrong notes, nothing off. The whole band is synchronized perfection.

Death is my only friend

The one that walks with me

To the end

I don't have anything

That money can buy today

The razor

I would have sworn I could see women crying in the front row as we brought the song to all its full glory. I could see Elias and Abel both grinning as I took their baby to another level. I grabbed the microphone stand and pulled myself up, and we tore into "Rip Out My Heart".

Misty slashed across the strings, pin-wheeling her arms as the boys added a mean double rhythm under her playing. Track after track, the whole show was flawless. Pyrotechnics went off correctly and on time to Metal Insanity as the boys leaped off side by side ramps, sliding across the floor.

We took the first bow and waved goodbye. The entire building was shaking as over twelve hundred fans were jumping up and down, banging on anything that made noise and trying to get us back to the stage. Everyone high fived backstage before we ran out and encores with "Cut The Chains" and "That Bitch". The place came unglued as we finished and headed back off the stage. The house lights came up as fans howled and screamed from behind the curtain wanting us back. Abel gave me the most wicked grin of his life.

"That is what I am fucking talking about! Now do you see Rhi?" he asked.

Champagne was brought in along with flowers. We all lifted a glass to celebrate. The owners of the Fillmore came back and whispered into Royston's ear. Royston shakes their hands.

"I'll send over the contracts in the morning," he told them.

I started screaming excitedly, throwing my arms around the boys and the band. Everyone was beaming. It was perfect. We stayed backstage for a while until the crowd thinned out. Security was still heavy at both ends of the alleyway as we opened the stage door and started lugging our gear out. Fans piled on either side trying to get a glimpse. Suddenly, I heard a familiar whistling coming across the stage. Royston looks at me and darted inside, bringing a young man in his late teens outside. I could see the kid was shaken.

"I'm sorry. I didn't mean to offend anyone; this guy was backstage standing next to me whistling that song. It got stuck in my head, that's all," he said.

I felt a shiver run up my back.

"Did you by any chance get a look at the fellow?

180

We were wondering if it was one of our friends late to the show?" he asked the kid.

Scratching his head he said, "Not really."

"All I can tell you is that he was wearing a funny hat like a derby or a bowler and a dark like tweed jacket or something. The hat was pulled low and with the way the lights were flashing and all the other effects, I couldn't really see his face," he replied.

"Sorry to trouble you, but thank you anyways," Royston replied politely, let the stagehand get back to work, and turned back to us.

"It might be a coincidence."

"And you don't believe it for a minute," I argued.

"I'm afraid not." Royston shook his head.

"That's what I thought," I said, punching him lightly.

Misty just shook her head and rubbed her arms.

I told everyone, "Let's go home. I need a cold beer and a final night with everyone."

Royston jumped in the tour bus as the rest of us got in our cars. The ride back was quiet, and the moon shined on the bay as we crossed the bridge.

"Do you think we will get more answers about that whistler guy?" Misty asked.

"I don't know. Apparently, we don't have all the

facts yet." Misty gave my thigh a playful squeeze and I reciprocated.

~Epilogue~

~The Dry Savages~

It seems, as one becomes older,
That the past has another pattern, and ceases to be a
mere sequence-
Or even development: the latter a partial fallacy
Encouraged by superficial notions of evolution,
Which becomes, in the popular mind, a means of
disowning the past.
The moments of happiness - not the sense of well-

being,
Fruition, fulfillment, security or affection,
Or even a very good dinner, but the sudden
illumination—
We had the experience but missed the meaning,
And approach to the meaning restores the experience
In a different form, beyond any meaning
We can assign to happiness. I have said before
That the past experience revived in the meaning
Is not the experience of one life only
But of many generations - not forgetting

Excerpt from Four Quartets by T.S. Elliot

Misty~ As with any beginning there is the ending. The poignant moments when we have to let something go in the hope that it will return one day. The next day the sun rose and we rolled out of bed, but there was a heaviness around the house and all of us. It felt like a lead weight was tied to our necks, it was like an unsaid word or phrase that no one wanted to utter.

Similar to T.S. Eliot poem Four Quartets when he took a long look at spirituality and meaning. How certain passages resonate with the reader, so much that they do something with them. I tattooed certain passages and phrases on my body from Melville and Eliot. The poet had such a profound effect on my thinking and blew away my senses every time I read his work.

More than a few customers came in requesting to have "I have measured out my life with coffee spoons" etched into their skin, so I wasn't the only one that thought that or was perhaps a tad crazy. Mad as a hatter perhaps, but we all have a little crazy in us, just varying degrees of insanity that's all.

We all gathered at our house for a final toast before we went our separate ways. The boys were unusually reserved allowing Royston and Rhianna to lead the festivities. Each of us were going back to our realities, but after the experience, I wasn't sure I wanted to stay in Los Angeles anymore. Rhianna was my girl and I belonged by her side.

The band was going to take off that was for sure, I would have to hire others to work my shop and

Nicki could run things while I toured. There were worse things in life then being successful, and I had found my happiness. We all had, there wasn't a dour face in the room. I looked around at all of us that were gathered and all I saw was smiles. Smiles from my chosen family.

There were no egos or hurt feelings, a lot of bridges had been mended and we had done something big, something kick ass that would stay with us forever. It was what we all wanted and it had finally happened. We had a hell of a life ahead of us and we would stay on the roller coaster as long as we could. I couldn't stop smiling at all of them as we gathered for one final group hug. Even baby Mia squealed at the end smiling and cooing in Gia's arms. I knew I would see the boys and girls again. My band was my family and we were tight. It just seemed like a chapter of our lives was closing for a moment. I hoped it would continue on some day if we were all willing…

~The End~

A note from the author:

Want more of your favorite characters? Go check out the following to get more inside info about the cast of Shadow & Flame:

For more reading on Elias & Genevieve, check out *Cain: Sins of the Father* and *Cain: Rage of Angels* by Elias Raven. You can find them all on Elias's Amazon page:

For more about Abel & Gia, see Gina Whitney's *Rocker Series (Books 1-3)- Saving Abel, Forgiving Gia, & Avenging Us*. Gina can be found on her Amazon page as well:

And, of course, you can see them in the rest of The Collective series' books also.